"I got you, Izzie. I'll get you through this."

She sagged against him, letting him take her weight and her fear and her sorrow. He took it all, standing solid as Black Mountain as he cradled her. She finally reined herself in and straightened to find both her brothers staring at them from across the yard. She stepped back from Clay and he cast a glance over his shoulder. Then he returned his attention to her.

"You going to be all right?"

She didn't think so. Everything around her seemed to be breaking loose and she couldn't hold the pieces together any longer. She should go and reassure the boys. Tell them that everything was all right. But it wasn't all right. It was so *not* all right.

HUNTER MOON

—

JENNA KERNAN

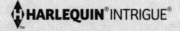

For Jim, always.

Recycling programs
for this product may
not exist in your area.

ISBN-13: 978-0-373-74936-2

Hunter Moon

This edition published by arrangement with Harlequin Books S.A.

For questions and comments about the quality of this book,
please contact us at CustomerService@Harlequin.com.

® and TM are trademarks of Harlequin Enterprises Limited or its
corporate affiliates. Trademarks indicated with ® are registered in the
United States Patent and Trademark Office, the Canadian Intellectual
Property Office and in other countries.

Printed in U.S.A.

www.Harlequin.com

Jenna Kernan has penned over two dozen novels and has received two RITA® Award nominations. Jenna is every bit as adventurous as her heroines. Her hobbies include recreational gold prospecting, scuba diving and gem hunting. Jenna grew up in the Catskills and currently lives in the Hudson Valley of New York State with her husband. Follow Jenna on Twitter, @jennakernan, on Facebook or at jennakernan.com.

Visit the Author Profile page at Harlequin.com for more titles.

CAST OF CHARACTERS

Clay Cosen—This former Shadow Wolf now works for the general livestock manager and is the best tracker on the rez. But his former gang affiliations rub many the wrong way. His job impounding free-roaming cattle puts him at odds with many ranchers, including Isabella Nosie. Yet, when someone threatens Izzie, he will do what is necessary to keep her safe.

Isabella (Izzie) Nosie—This cattle rancher was engaged to Clay's best friend before his murder. Her grazing permits are the envy of many. Now someone is cutting her fences and killing her cattle. Is it the competition, rustlers or something much more deadly?

Floyd Patch—Just a fellow cattle rancher who has asked Izzie out on several occasions. How far is he willing to go to get what he's after?

Arnold Tessay—He is a tribal council member who works with Clay's brother Clyne in tribal government. Is Arnold a pillar of their community or a wolf in sheep's clothing?

Boone Pizarro—The tribe's livestock coordinator. Is his order to pull Izzie's grazing permits in the tribe's best interest or his own?

Dale Donner—Tribal general livestock manager for Black Mountain and Clay's boss, but some of his decisions seem questionable. Is he working for the tribe or the cartels?

Ruben Fox—An Apache gang member connected to the cartel drug trade. Is Ruben trying to warn Clay or set him up for another fall?

Glendora Clawson—Clay's grandmother. She now has proof that her granddaughter survived the crash that killed her daughter. She wants her grandsons to find their missing sister, Jovanna, and return her in time to undergo the Apache Sunrise Ceremony of womanhood.

Clyne Cosen—Clay's oldest brother is a member of the Apache Tribal Council and a retired, wounded war veteran.

Gabe Cosen—The second oldest brother, Gabe is chief of the tribal police on Black Mountain.

Kino Cosen—Clay's younger brother is on his honeymoon while searching for their missing little sister.

Luke Forrest—An Apache FBI agent and the Cosen brothers' uncle. Some say Luke is a traitor for joining the feds. Would an Apache man willing to work for the government also be willing to work for the cartels?

Chapter One

Black Mountain Apache Reservation

Izzie Nosie lay low over the mare's neck hoping to make herself less of a target for whoever was shooting at her.

Damn, this was her land.

What was going on?

Her legs flapped as she kicked her chestnut quarter horse, Biscuit, to greater speeds. Who was up there shooting at her?

She leaned to the right, touching the leather bridle to her horse's strong neck. The signal was received, and Biscuit darted between two pines, jumping the downed log that blocked escape. She knew her pursuers were not on horseback, so she did her best to take the route hardest to maneuver on foot. Still, she couldn't outrun a bullet. The next shot hit the tree to her left, sending shards of bark and splintered wood flying out against her cheek, barely missing her eye. She ignored the sting, focusing on flight.

Just a little farther and she'd be below range. She knew the terrain as well as she knew the layout of her barn. Fifty feet more and she could cut down a sharp hill and be clear. It'd take them a few minutes to reach the embankment for another shot, and she meant to be long gone by then. She broke from the woods and right into the path of another gunman. This one was mounted on a tall buckskin.

She drew up short, causing poor Biscuit to rear back as her mare tried to go from a gallop to a stop and nearly made it. The rider was Indian, big, lean and aiming a rifle. She used a trick of her ancestors, throwing her near leg over the pommel and falling until she lay pressed to Biscuit's opposite side. Her fingers gripped the coarse hair of her mare's neck, and she squeezed the pommel with her upper knee to keep from tumbling to the ground.

"Izzie. It's me. Clay Cosen."

She felt her already galloping heart pound painfully as emotion bled through her. What was Clay doing here? Was he one of them?

No. Never. But the doubt lifted its head like a rattlesnake in a bed of bluebonnets. Her mother's words echoed in her mind.

He's a convicted criminal.

"This way," he called. "I've got a truck."

She hesitated just long enough to cause him to look back. She saw his face go hard. Somehow he knew at a glance that she no longer trusted him. His tight, guarded expression filled her with regrets. So many regrets.

"You coming?"

Emotion paralyzed her, and she lost her balance, slipping from her saddle and tumbling along the ground. The jolt of pain made her suck wind between her teeth. She fell, rolling to her feet. Clay was there, rifle gripped in one hand and the other extended out to her, as he guided his horse with only the pressure of his legs. She knew the man could ride. His rodeo titles proved that, and he was a sight to see approaching at a full gallop. She didn't think. She just acted, grasping his gloved hand as he charged by and leaped into the air as he pulled. He swung her up behind him. His horse never broke stride as he continued on, down the embankment. Behind them one more shot sounded.

Then they were racing over her pasture and down the steep incline. She could not see past his slate-gray cowboy hat and broad shoulders sheathed in a navy blue gingham check. He wore a battered leather vest the color of his horse, work gloves and faded denim jeans over cowboy boots that had seen better days.

Izzie wrapped her arms about his narrow waist and glanced behind them. There came Biscuit, galloping after her mistress. Izzie looked beyond but saw no one step from the cover of the aspen and pines and heard no more gunshots.

Her ears buzzed, and she trembled as the adrenaline ebbed. Izzie gave herself permission to hold him again and pressed a cheek to Clay's back. The horse's breath sounded like a great bellows as they charged on and on through the tall, yellowing grass. She held tight, feeling the taut muscles of his abdomen beneath her splayed fingers. Their bodies moved together with the horse, rocking, and Izzie closed her eyes and savored this moment, because, regardless of the reason, it had brought Clay back into her arms again.

It wasn't until his mount began to slow and Clay's posture became more erect that her mind reengaged.

Why was Clay Cosen here in her pasture? How could she know that he was not with them? But instead of thinking, she had just jumped right into his arms like the damn fool she always was every time she got around this particular man.

Poison, that's what her mother, Carol Nosie, called him. The kind of man to ruin a girl and not just her reputation. Look what Clay's father had done to his poor mother. A cautionary tale of the consequences that came of choosing the wrong kind of man. This one would take everything, her position in the community, her self-respect, her obligations to her family and, most importantly, her heart.

So why did holding him again feel so right?

Izzie's hands slipped from his middle, paused for one instant on his hips and then let go.

Clay twisted and glanced back at her.

"You okay?"

What kind of a question was that? She'd been shot at, lost her seat and then her horse and now sat tucked against his body as if she belonged to him.

"Hell, no, I'm not all right."

Clay made a sound that might have been a laugh. Then he turned the horse, so they could see the way they had come. Biscuit was trailing her at a trot.

"I don't see any sign of them." He glanced back at her, giving her an enticing view of his strong jawline and the slight stubble that already grew there. His russet skin was so beautiful, taut and tanned. Izzie lifted her hand and had it halfway to his cheek when she realized what she was doing and forced it back down.

"Who were they?" asked Clay.

"No idea. I noticed I was missing cattle and thought they got up into the woods. There's another small pasture up in that draw. But the next thing I know, I see someone on foot, and when I called out, the idiot started shooting at me."

"I'd say at least two idiots from the sound of the shots. One was using a semiautomatic weapon."

Her body went cold at that news.

He scowled at her, and still he was a welcome sight. His expression was a mix of concern and aggravation, as if she had intentionally put herself in danger.

Clay had been born a month earlier to the day, but at twenty-four, she no longer needed him shepherding her, did she?

"You're bleeding," he said and leaned in her direction. She held still as he removed one glove and swiped a thumb gently over the crest of her cheek. She felt the sting of pain, and his fingers came away bloody. He held her chin and tilted her head as if she were a child. Well, they weren't thirteen anymore, and he was not hers. So why was it so hard to draw back?

"It's fine."

Clay motioned with his head. "Let's go."

They rode at a canter across the pasture, and she noted her herd had moved far down field. Good, she thought. Farther away from the bullets. That's all she needed—dead cows. It was hard enough to make ends meet with the water restrictions.

"Why are you here, Cosen?" she asked, refusing herself the intimacy of his first name.

He pointed to a truck parked along her fence line. "Collecting strays."

Clay worked for Dale Donner, the general livestock coordinator. One of their jobs was gathering strays from all reservation highways, which included this out-of-the-way road snaking along her grazing land. But she kept her fences in good repair, mostly because she could not afford to lose any cattle. Yet he was here, working. Her mouth went dry.

"Strays?" she repeated.

Her cattle were the only ones up here, and she was missing more than a few. Izzie had a sick feeling in her stomach.

"You catch any?"

His expression was serious. "Some."

"How many?"

"Izzie, someone just shot at you. I'd feel a whole lot better if we had this conversation out of range and behind cover. I've got room in my trailer for Biscuit."

He remembered the name of her favorite horse. What else did he remember? Their first kiss? The night she let him go a little too far? Or the day she told him she could not see him anymore?

They rode through her downed fence, the wire lying on the ground. She didn't see any cattle on the road, but she swung down to lift the wire.

"It's been cut," she said.

He dismounted, too, glancing back toward the woods, his rifle still out and ready.

"Get behind the trailer."

"The fence," she said.

"The hell with the fence."

"Did you do this?" she asked.

In answer, his color rose and his jaw set. Then he grabbed her with more force than necessary and hustled her over to the horse trailer.

Clay opened the gate and lowered the ramp. She loaded Biscuit and exited the trailer to find his mount tied to the ring on the side of the trailer. She watched him disconnect the trailer hitch.

He jerked his head toward the truck. "Get in, Bella."

He hadn't called her that since her sophomore year in high school on the night she told him she must stop seeing him.

Why, Bella? Why?

Clay rounded the trailer, and she heard the gate shut with a resounding clang.

"I can't leave Biscuit."

Clay took hold of her arm and muscled her along. He was much bigger and stronger than she recalled. He had to release her or the gun to get the door open, and he chose her. He motioned to the interior, and she slipped into the cab. Then he jogged around the front of the grille and slid the rifle into place on the rack behind them.

She caught the movement and shouted.

"There!" she said, pointing.

Someone moved on the top of the tree line. Clay leaped into his seat and started the truck, accelerating into the U-turn and narrowly missing the opposite ditch.

They traveled a half mile down the hill before he lifted the radio from his hip.

"My brothers are coming. Don't want them riding into gunfire."

She nodded her agreement to that. He must mean Gabe and Kino. Gabe was the new chief, and Kino was now a police officer for the tribal police. Izzie had heard that Clay's little brother was about to be married.

Clay called his office, relayed the details and clipped the radio to his belt. He glanced in the side mirror and then back to the road. "Who are they?"

She shook her head. "I don't know. I didn't get a good look." She dabbed at her cheek and winced. The blood was already drying on her face. "Why would men with automatic rifles be sneaking around in those woods?"

"A good question," he said. "What's up there?"

"Just another pasture. Oh, and a road. The tribe just improved it. It's gravel now. They did a really nice job."

"Why would the tribe improve a road going to pastureland?"

Izzie wrinkled her brow as she thought about that. "I don't know."

"It's just an open field?" he asked.

"Well, there's some dry fill up beyond the pasture, some digging. The tribe uses the dirt to fill holes. Maybe that's why they need the road. To bring in bigger equipment?"

"Maybe."

But he didn't sound convinced, and his tone made her realize she should know what was happening on the land she leased. Izzie needed to get some answers.

Chapter Two

Clay had sworn he'd never be back here.

But here he was, sitting in the police station interview room. The room that he had hoped to never see the inside of again. The very same room where he had been brought in handcuffs. Had it really been eight years? Seemed like yesterday.

Clay felt the sheen of cold sweat cover him, and he tried to tell himself that this was different.

Was it? Or was he in that kind of trouble all over again?

They had met the authorities at the bottom of the pasture. After the tribal police had cleared the scene and found no sign of the gunmen, one of Gabe's officers had taken Clay's rifle, and they had told Izzie that fifty-one of her cows had been impounded for trespass on tribal lands by a representative of the General Livestock Coordinator—in other words, by Clay. After hearing that news, Izzie hadn't spoken to him once on the long drive to the station, and he expected that she'd never speak to him again. That realization was more disturbing than sitting in this damned room again.

But he hadn't done anything wrong. Unless he had. You didn't have to know it to have done it. He'd learned that lesson well enough. Maybe this was just like the last time, only it was Izzie setting him up. Letting the cows out, calling the manager's number, drawing him into a gunfight.

No, that was just crazy, his stupid paranoid fears rearing up like a horse in the shoot at a rodeo. Tighten the cinch. Open the gate. Watch it buck. Eight seconds and all you could do was hold on. Clay held on now. He'd tried to make the right decisions. Tried to think before he acted. Tried not to take everything at face value, not be so gullible. But when he'd seen Izzie running for her life, he hadn't thought about the consequences. He had just ridden full speed into gunfire.

Clay rested his head in his hands and drew a deep breath. He still felt sick to his stomach.

He'd asked Gabe to call his boss and tell him where he was. Clay knew that if there was even a whiff of misdeeds, Donner would fire him. He'd do anything to keep this job. Anything.

He'd been lucky to get hired in the first place—with unemployment so high on the Rez and so many men searching for honest work, men without his priors.

His younger brother, Kino, came in to speak to

him. Kino had been on the force about a year, acting as a patrolman. It was something Clay could never be. They didn't take men with criminal records into the police or the FBI, where his uncle Luke Forrest worked. Kino had been surprised that they had let Clay work with the Shadow Wolves on Immigration and Customs Enforcement. But Clay was a special case because he was Native American, which was a requirement, a very good tracker and his conviction was not a felony. Though it nearly had been.

"So, busy day?" asked Kino, taking a seat and opening his laptop.

Clay didn't laugh. The last time he was here, Kino had been thirteen years old.

What was his boss going to say? He'd sent him to clear strays and he'd ended up in jail, again.

"Where's Izzie?"

Kino thumbed over his shoulder. "Captain's office."

"You mean Gabe's office."

"I call him captain here. We only have one interrogation room."

Clay knew that.

"She says you had no right to impound her cattle."

"They were on the road."

"She's claiming that they were released."

"Upper fences were cut," said Clay.

"Yeah, I heard that."

"I *saw* that. Don't know about the lower pasture. I didn't see anything, but I wasn't looking."

"We'll check. You didn't cut them, did you?"

Clay blinked in astonishment, expecting Kino to laugh or smile or say this was some joke. He didn't. He just sat there, waiting.

"No."

"I think all our guys are up in the woods," said Kino. "I'll ask them to run the fence lines."

"They're going to ruin the scene."

"You and I are not the only ones who know how to track, brother."

Clay nodded.

"So you want to do this, or would you prefer one of the other guys handled it?"

"No. Go on."

His kid brother asked the questions, and Clay answered. He'd picked up four truckloads of cattle with Roger Tolino. They'd gotten a second call about cattle on the upper road. He'd sent Roger back with the cattle truck. Clay had found the cut fence after Roger left.

"Clean cut. All three lines, right by the post." Clay had searched the ground. "One man was wearing boots, weight about two-fifty, judging from the depth of the tracks and recovery of the grass inside the tread." He had seen the strays and thought it easier to just steer them back into the pasture. He was just repairing the fences when he'd heard the first shots. "I couldn't call it in because there's no cell service up there." So he'd used his radio. Called Veronica in the office and asked her to call Gabe.

Getting his statement took a while because Kino had to type his replies. Clay waited as Kino pecked away on the laptop, feeling like a damned fool. Eventually, Kino closed the computer and regarded Clay.

"You didn't do anything wrong," said Kino.

"That's what I thought the last time."

Kino nodded. "You really didn't know what they were doing?"

Clay stared at his kid brother in astonishment and then realized they had never spoken of the crime.

"Who?" asked Clay, making sure he wasn't talking about today.

"Martin and Rubin."

"Martin said he wanted some pop. I stopped. They went in. I waited. They came out, and I drove away."

"Just like that. Didn't you see the blood on Martin's shirt?"

Kino stared. Clay knew what he was thinking. His older brother was guilty or he was a fool. Clay never liked the choice. He lowered his head. "Are we finished?"

Kino stood. "Yeah. Sure. So, I'll see you Saturday?"

Clay rose. "Saturday?"

Kino's voice held impatience. "The wedding?"

Clay's mouth dropped open as he realized he'd forgotten. His kid brother was getting married and then honeymooning in the Badlands of South Dakota, so he could pick up the trail of their missing little sister.

"Yeah, of course. Sorry. My mind is just… Like you said, long day."

Kino walked him out.

"Want to go for a beer after work?" asked Clay.

Kino rubbed his neck. "Sorry. Can't. Wedding stuff."

"Oh, right. Well, see you Saturday."

"Don't forget the barbecue. Thursday night. Rehearsal and dinner at Salt River on Friday."

Clay nodded and left the station, shedding the stale heated atmosphere for the crisp air of a perfect September day. Relief poured down on him with the sunshine. He looked to the west, to Black Mountain. Emerald-green Ponderosa pines that were broken by patches of brilliant yellow aspen ringed the base. Nearer the top, forest gave way to the browning grass. The crown looked as if someone had scraped away all vegetation. This was where the reservation got its name, from the dark of the tallest mountain in Arizona. Eleven thousand two hundred and twenty feet. On this cool day, the crown looked black against the bright blue sky, but soon the snow would cover it again. He'd been to the windy peak. All Apache boys climbed it. There, on the top the Crown Spirits lived. *The Gaan*, as his people call them, had been sent by the Creator to teach them to live in harmony.

When Clay told outsiders he was Black Mountain Apache, they assumed he lived in the desert and wore a red head scarf and a long belted shirt. The truth was that he did wear a red kerchief, but about his neck, and his reservation was mountainous with a ski resort in addition to a casino. They had plenty of lakes and some of the best trout fishing and elk hunting anywhere. But mostly what they had was the grassland, and much of it had been broken into permitted grazing areas. Raising cattle was still big business here. Some pastures had been in certain families for generations. Like Isabella Nosie's grazing rights. It had been her grandfather's and her father's—William's—and now it was hers for as long as she kept filling out the application.

Some folks thought that system unfair. That they should have a lottery. Clay had no cattle, so he stayed out of the debate.

He took one final look back at the station. Was she still in there?

Clay had missed Isabella more than he'd ever admit. She came to him in dreams sometimes, and on a good day he might see her in town. He'd caught her looking back at him once, but she never spoke to him. He didn't blame her. Lots of folks looked right through him now. Or they hurried the other way as if he was contagious.

Clay recovered the truck he drove for his job, headed back to the offices and checked in with Dale Donner. Besides managing the communal cattle and horse herds, Donner's offices collected fines, cared for impounded livestock and sold unclaimed stock at auction. That meant showing up in tribal court and dealing with the tribe's various livestock associations over disputes. Donner was also on the tribe's general livestock board, along with Boone Pizzaro, Franklin Soto and two members of the tribal council. Boone Pizarro was the general livestock coordinator, in charge of managing the tribe's cattle holdings including all grazing permits issued to ranchers on the reservation. Franklin Soto oversaw the health of the herds on the Rez and made sure all Black Mountain cattle complied with regulations with the state's livestock sanitary board.

Clay drove the two blocks, parked and entered Donner's office. He felt as if he had been away for a week.

Donner did not glance up as Clay came to a stop before the battered wooden desk littered with piles of paper. His boss was a barrel-chested Apache with dark braided hair that framed a face deeply lined and aged by the sun to the color of a well-oiled saddle. He seemed perpetually impatient with the stupidity of both his cattle and his men. Behind him, various clipboards hung on nails beside a calendar featuring a large longhorn steer's photo. On the lower half of the calendar, Donner had crossed off all the days in the month up to and including today, Monday, September 7.

His boss glanced up, and his flint eyes fixed on Clay.

"We registered fifty-one cows with Nosie's brand," said Donner.

"There were four more, but I shooed them back into their pasture. Mr. Donner, those fences on the upper pasture were cut."

Donner lowered the clipboard. "What do you mean cut?"

"I mean with a wire cutter. Someone came in from the road, parked, cut the fences and left."

"What about the lower pasture?"

"I didn't see anything, but I was pretty busy rounding up cattle."

"Well, heck. We got to call your brother about that."

"Didn't he call you?" Had Gabe forgotten to alert his boss?

"Yup. Said you'd been delayed."

Clay realized Donner didn't know about what happened with Izzie and the shooters. It took several minutes to relate the story, and his boss's mouth hung open for most of it. Clay didn't think he'd ever talked so much in his life. Except that day in court. When he finished, his shoulders sagged.

"Well, a heck of a day." Donner sat back and scratched his head, sending one of his long graying braids wiggling. "I'll call Pizzaro and Bustros. Update them and have them take a look at the fences and the cattle."

Victor Bustros was not technically on the general livestock board, but worked under Pizarro, the livestock coordinator. Bustros's title was livestock brand inspector. Because of the record keeping of individual brands, Bustros had a clerk who helped him keep up with the paperwork. Bustros's job also including overseeing the weekly cattle auctions.

Cattle were still the tribe's main source of income, though tourism was catching up. These four men—Bustros, Pizzaro, Soto and his boss, Donner—held positions of importance in this enterprise overseeing the care, business and health of the tribe's holdings. Clay felt lucky to work with them. Now Clay hoped that his actions today had not jeopardized that.

"Sir, would you like me to have a look at Nosie's lower pasture?"

"Leave that to your brothers. If what you say is true, that might be a crime scene."

If it were true? Clay felt his face heat. Even after six-and-a-half spotless years of work, his boss did not take his word at face value.

If the impounded stock hadn't belonged to Izzie, then Clay would have let it go. But instead, he opened his mouth again.

"Sir, I could…"

Donner's gaze snapped to his, and he gave a slow shake of his head. It was a gesture Clay recognized as a warning. Clay closed his mouth.

"You've done enough."

Clay accepted the long, hard look Donner gave him.

"Finish your paperwork before you leave."

Knowing he'd been dismissed, Clay returned to his desk in the outer office to wake up his ancient computer. An hour later he had his hat back on his head and was leaving for the day.

Clyne and Gabe, his older brothers, still lived in their grandmother Glendora's place. But he and Kino had a small house outside of Black River, one of four towns on the reservation and the one that housed the tribal headquarters. Since Kino and Lea Altaha would like their own place, Clay planned to move back to his grandmother's while they waited for placement. It could take over a year for the newlyweds to get their house through the tribe's housing organization, and Clay recognized that they needed privacy.

Clay climbed into his own truck, which was older, smaller and dustier than the one he used for tribe business. He drove by his grandmother's house, knowing he was always welcome for dinner. But the prospect of telling his story one more time did not appeal, and so he skipped the chance at the best fry bread in Black Mountain in favor of frozen pizza and privacy. Since Kino would be out, there might still be one last beer in the frig.

When he pulled in the driveway, he realized he wasn't getting that pizza or that beer or any peace, because Izzie Nosie stood, leaning against her pickup with her arms folded beneath her beautiful bosom. She looked ready for battle.

She lifted her chin as he stepped out of his truck. Was it only a few hours ago that she had clung to him while they raced together across the wide stretch of open pasture?

"Izzie, what are you doing here?"

"I want to know who let my cows out."

"I'll bet."

"You are the best tracker on this reservation. So I want to hire you, Cosen."

Clay could only imagine how hard it was for her to ask the likes of him for help.

"You might be better to ask Kino or Gabe. They're the investigators."

"And they *are* investigating. But I want someone who is looking out for my interests. That's you."

"That's a conflict of interest, Izzie. Or did you forget that I work for the livestock manager?"

Her eyebrows rose. "Still?"

That stung. "You think he fired me? For what, doing my job?"

She held on to her scowl, but her cheeks flushed a becoming rose. Then she pressed a finger into his chest. "You should have told me that my cows were on the highway, Cosen."

"They pay me to collect them. Not to contact the owners."

"Do you know how much it will cost me to get them out?" She ticked off the amounts on her fingers. "Gathering fee, five dollars a head. That's two-hundred and sixty dollars, and that's only if I can sell some cows and get that money to them in twenty-four hours, which I can't. Then it's two dollars a day per cow for every day you have them. That's a hundred and four dollars more."

"Izzie, your strays were scattered all over the highway."

"Cosen, my fences are good. I need you to help me prove that, so I can appeal."

He leaned against his truck, trying to think,

but his eyes kept dipping to her lovely face and those soft lips. Izzie's hair was dark brown, and she often wore it pulled back to reveal her small, perfectly shaped ears and long, slender neck. She knew he liked her hair loose; it was loose now and had been recently combed. She wore pink lip gloss that made her full mouth look ripe and tempting.

Clay frowned.

She lifted her pointed chin, and her fine brows rose. She rested a hand on his chest. His heartbeat accelerated and his skin tingled. He had to force himself not to reach out and gather her in his arms.

He stared down at her hand, fingers splayed across his chest, the left ring finger still somehow bare. Then he followed the slim line of her arm to her narrow shoulders. Her soft hair brushed her collarbone, and she wore no jewelry except the gold crucifix about her neck, the one her father had given her at her first communion. Her face was heart-shaped and her upper lip more full than the bottom, giving the impression that she was forever freshly kissed. Her skin was soft brown, and her eyes sloped downward at the corners. He stared a moment at the light brown eyes that were flecked with gold, but it was like looking at the sun—dangerous and alluring all at once.

He knew what she wanted, and it wasn't him.

But his body still remembered her touch. And the memories of her threatened to make him do something stupid, like risk his job for this woman.

"You haven't spoken to me in seven years," he said. "Now you're asking for my help?"

A STAB OF guilt spiked inside Izzie, and she couldn't hold his gaze. He was right. She'd avoided him and the scorn she knew would come by association. This was a small community. A person's place in the tribe depended on many things—character, family and who you chose to love. Loving Clay had cost too much. So she had let him go. Now she wanted a favor. She thought of her two little brothers and stiffened her spine. Then she met the accusation in his gaze.

"I'm asking," she said.

He exhaled loudly through his nose. "Izzie, I need this job. I won't do anything to jeopardize it."

"And I'm not asking you to. Just take a look at the tracks."

He was staring at her again, debating. She saw it now. The anger in his stance and the unwillingness.

"Call Gabe. He's the chief of police."

"I want someone who is working for me—not the tribe. Plus he made it very clear that I'm a suspect in whatever is going on up there."

"You?" He laughed right in her face. The sound was hard. "Isabella Nosie? The girl with all As in high school. The good girl, sings in the choir, took over for her dad, helps raise her brothers and has never made a mistake in her life?"

That was just one step too far. She planted a fist on her hip.

"I made *one*."

His laughter died and their eyes met. She read the hurt in his expression as her words hit their target. They both knew the mistake she meant. She had loved him.

Clay sagged back against the truck bed as if she'd slapped him. Izzie felt terrible.

"I'm sorry, Clay. I didn't mean it." Actually, going out with Clay had been the best thing that ever happened to her. Until she'd let her parents run him off. Why hadn't she stood up for herself?

Because she'd been sixteen with dreams of college and a career, and, after his mom had been killed by that drunk driver, Clay was so angry and reckless, she barely recognized him. Then her father got sick and she'd made that promise. The next thing she knew, she had become responsible for her brothers and mother, and now she might lose it all.

"Will you help me?" she asked.

"No."

"Fine. Then I'll just do it myself."

She turned to go, and he captured her wrist. She paused and he released her.

Clay removed his hat and struck it against his leg. His face went bright, with two streaks of color across his prominent cheekbones. Did that mean he did care what happened to her? Her heart fluttered at the possibility, and she cursed herself for a fool.

Clay regrouped, releasing her as he looked down his broad straight nose at her. He was scowling now and his nostrils flared. He'd never looked more handsome.

Clay didn't wear his hair long, like his brothers Kino and Clyne. Neither did he wear it buzzed short like Gabe. Clay chose a length that was neither fashionable, functional nor traditional. His black hair ended bluntly at his strong jaw-line with bangs that he either swept back or let fall over his piercing eyes. His brow was prominent and his eyebrows thick. His black lashes were long and framed his deep brown eyes. She'd always wondered why he didn't recognize his model good looks, but Clay seemed unaware of how he turned heads.

She met his hard stare, gnawing on her lower lip.

"If you are involved with anything illegal up there, you best tell me right now."

She gaped as the shock hit her like a slap. He

couldn't really think she had anything to do with this. Could he?

He looked serious enough. "Because I will not be dragged into another mess."

"I'm not involved with anything illegal."

He continued to stare, lips pressed thin and colorless.

She threw up her hands in disgust. "Okay! I swear! I'm not involved in anything, and all I know is someone cut my fences, half my herd is gone, I'm missing cattle and now I owe a fine."

"What is it you want me to do, exactly?" he asked.

"Check the fields for tracks. Tell me everything you can. Maybe poke around in the upper pasture."

"The crime scene, you mean."

"Yes."

"How much?"

"Fifty bucks?"

He shook his head. "I want a cow for my sister's Sunrise Ceremony."

"Your sister?" Some of the fight drained out of her, replaced by shock. Izzie touched the gold crucifix, rubbing it between her thumb and index finger before letting it drop. "I thought Jovanna was..."

"So did we. She's not. Just missing. We are going to find her."

Izzie absorbed that bit of news. It was really none of her business, but she remembered the bright and happy little girl who left with her mother for her first contest and never came back. If they could find her, they'd need every bit of that cow to feed all the company and relatives who would attend. A homecoming and a Sunrise Ceremony. Goodness, there would be hundreds of people.

"She's been gone a long time," said Izzie.

Clay said nothing to that.

"All right, then."

He replaced his hat. They were close to a deal. Once she'd known him intimately. But then he had been a boy. This man before her had become a stranger.

He made a sound of frustration in his throat.

When he met her gaze, she braced, knowing he had reached a decision. And also knowing that once Clay Cosen settled on a course it was nearly impossible to change his mind.

Chapter Three

When he finally spoke, his voice was tight, clipped and frosty as the snow off Black Mountain.

"All right. One cow. My pick."

It took a moment for Izzie to realize that she had won. She blinked up at Clay, recovered herself and nodded.

"My pick," he repeated. "And if you are lying to me or dragging me into something illegal, I will turn you over to Gabe so fast, little brothers or no little brothers."

It was a threat that hit home, for while her mother still ran the household, Izzie owned the cattle. It was a sticking point between her and her mother, for her father had left the entire herd to his eldest daughter instead of his wife. Her mother, a righteous woman with a knack for scripture, also had a habit of spending more than her husband could make. And though her father had had trouble telling his wife no, Izzie did not.

Which was why she had increased the herd by forty head and also why her mother was equally furious and proud of her. Izzie planned to keep her promise and pass her father's legacy to her brothers. Up until today she had done well. Up until today when she had lost fifty-one head. Her shoulders slumped a little, but she managed to keep her chin up.

"That's a deal." She stuck out her hand and pushed down the hope that he would take it.

He stared at her hand and then back to her and then back to her hand. Finally he clasped it. The contact was brief. But her reaction was not. She felt the tingle of his palm pressing to hers clear up to her jaw. Why, oh why did she have to have a thing for this man?

Clay broke the contact, leaving Izzie with her hand sticking out like a fool. Clay rubbed his palm on his thigh as if anxious to be rid of all traces of their touch. She scowled, recalling a time when things were different.

"When do we start?" she asked.

"Sooner is better. Tracks don't improve with time."

"Let's go, then. We can take my truck."

He hesitated, glancing to his vehicle. She followed his gaze, noticing he did not have a gun rack.

"You want to bring your rifle?"

"Don't carry one."

She frowned, thinking she had not heard him correctly. Clay hunted. He fished. Surely he had a rifle. It was part of life here. Shooting at coyotes and gophers and rattlesnakes, though she usually took a shovel to the snakes. Everyone she knew carried a firearm. But everyone she knew had not been charged with a crime.

He was allowed to carry one. His rescue earlier today proved that. Was it because he now knew the difference between robbery and armed robbery?

"What did you use earlier?"

"Belongs to the office."

She eyed him critically. He didn't just look different. He *was* different in ways she could only guess at.

"You don't hunt anymore?"

"Sometimes with my brothers. I mostly fish." He glanced away, and his hands slid into his back pockets as he rocked nervously from toe to heel, heel to toe.

Finally he looked up. She met Clay's gaze, and his expression gave nothing away.

"Still want my help?" he asked.

Izzie nodded.

He glanced toward his house, and she realized that he must not have eaten yet, since she'd caught him before he even made it to his front door.

"I'll buy you a burger after," she promised.

His mouth quirked. "Okay."

He strode past his battered pickup toward her newer-model Ram with the double wheels front and back and the trailer hitch behind. Oh, how her mother hated this truck, even though it was a used model.

Izzie watched Clay pass. His easy gait and graceful stride mesmerized her until she realized he was headed toward the driver's side. For a minute she thought he meant to drive. Izzie still had two years' worth of payments on her truck, and nobody drove it but her. But instead of taking the wheel, Clay opened her door for her and stepped back.

She felt her mouth drop open but managed to hold on as she nodded her thanks and swept inside the cab. He waited a moment and then closed the door before rounding the hood and removing his hat. Then he slid in beside her, hat in his lap. He fiddled with the seat controls, sending his seat as far back as it would go, and still his knees were flexed past ninety degrees. Then he sat motionless as she headed home.

"Who do you think cut your fences?" he asked as they rolled down the narrow mountain road from his place and toward hers out past Pinyon Lake. Here the forest lined both sides of the road with the pavement creating a narrow gap in the walls of pines.

"I have no idea."

"Anyone threatening you or trying to buy you out?"

"Buy me out, no." She remembered something, and she squeezed the wheel. "But my neighbor did ask me out a few times."

"Who?"

"Floyd."

Clay straightened. "Floyd Patch? He must be close to forty."

She and Clay were both twenty-four. He was born in February and she was born on the same day in March. There was a time she had joked that she liked older men. But that didn't seem funny right now.

"He's only thirty-six."

Clay rolled his eyes and brushed the crown of his felt hat, but said nothing. He considered the ceiling of the cab for a long moment. His usual posture, Izzie recalled, when he was thinking.

She smiled at the familiarity. It seemed that so much about him was the same. But not everything. Izzie steered them onto the main road, deciding to take the long way back to keep from the possibility of encountering her mother on the road. Izzie glanced at the clock, realizing her mother would likely be home because the boys should be climbing off the school's late bus about now. Clay's voice dragged her back to the present.

"Clyne said he was on the agenda a while back. I saw him talking to my boss a time ago about the tribe's communal pastures."

Who was he talking about?

"Which ones to close for renourishment."

Patch, she realized. Her neighbor.

"I heard Donner say that Patch was asking the council to impose a lottery for grazing permits again."

Izzie clenched the wheel. "But that doesn't make any sense. Lotteries mean ranchers might get grazing land clean on the other side of the reservation."

Clay shrugged. He had no horse in this particular race.

"You think Floyd wants my permits?"

"Don't know. But if he can't get the council to change the way permits are distributed, he could get them by marrying you."

Izzie let out a sound of frustration. "Those permits and the cattle don't belong to me. They are my brothers'."

"Whose name is on the permits?"

Izzie said nothing because they both knew that a minor could not own permits. Of course you had to be of age and Apache to even apply. As long as she didn't miss the October first application date, which she never did, then the permits were hers until her brother Will was old enough to apply in her place. That was the way it had always been. She hadn't come up with the system, but now she was starting to wonder if Floyd was indeed interested in her permits.

She turned on the cutoff that took her up the mountain, and Clay cast her a glance, wondering, no doubt, about her choice of routes. This way wasn't faster.

"Daylight is burning," he said.

"I know." She increased her speed and leaned forward, as if that would make them climb the hill quicker.

"Did you go out with him?"

She had to think for a minute about who he meant.

"No. No, of course not."

"He's got twice your herd."

"But not enough land to graze them. He'll have to sell some or apply for another permit."

"Or add them to the communal herd."

She and Clay shared a concerned look.

"Can you tell if he is the one who cut the fences?"

"Maybe." He toyed with his hat. "Let's start on the lower pasture?"

"Sure." She'd have to drive by the upper area where the shooting had been. Would the police still be there? "Then I want you to see the road and the place where the tribe is taking fill. They've leveled a wide area, for their trucks, I guess."

"To get at the hillside?"

"All they told me was that pasture permits didn't keep them from timbering the forest or exercising mineral rights. But this isn't timbering. Well, some is."

"What do you mean?"

"They aren't choosing which trees to take to thin the forest or clear the brush or whatever. They clear-cut a patch in the middle of the forest about fifty-by-fifty feet."

Clay frowned and rubbed the brim of his hat with his thumb and index finger, deep in thought.

Both she and Clay stretched their necks as they passed the new gravel road leading into the forest, but she saw nothing remarkable and no evidence of police activity. Whoever had shot at them was long gone. They passed the spot where his truck had been parked and arrived a few minutes later at the lower pasture, where most of her remaining cows milled close to the fence.

Izzie wished she had risked the shorter ride, as the sun was already descending toward sunset. It had been hard to give up the long days of August, but the air was already cool up here at the higher elevations, and so she shrugged into her denim coat, then realized Clay did not have one.

Clay pointed at her rifle, hooked neatly to her gun rack behind the seats.

"Take that," he said.

She did. He had told her to take one of her rifles but left the second firearm in place. Was that because he knew she was a better shot or for some other reason?

"You had a gun earlier," she said checking the load and adding a box of cartridges to her coat pocket for good measure.

"Have to. Part of my job." He tried to step past her. She blocked his path. He stopped and faced her.

"Why don't you own a gun, Clay?"

"No one wants to see an ex-con with a rifle in his hands."

"But you weren't charged with a felony. You are allowed to own one, right?"

"Right."

He raked his fingers past his temples and lowered his hat over his glossy black hair that brushed the collar of his shirt.

"Can we get started?"

She extended an arm in invitation. He continued, walking the highway, scanning the ground.

"Do you think the police are done investigating up there?" she asked, indicating the site of the shooting. "I didn't see any activity."

"For the day, maybe. But I'm not poking around in their crime scene."

Clay already had his eyes on the ground; she kept hers on the trees far above them, perhaps two miles away. For a shot you would need a scope and some luck to make the target. But still she held her rifle ready as she searched for more gunmen.

She followed behind him as he walked the highway. No one drove past. This road was too far from anything or anyone and was rarely used, except for today, of course.

Clay headed toward the pasture, and all the curious cows that had crowded the fence line fled in the opposite direction. She resisted the urge to count them.

He had already stepped through the fencing and stood lifting the upper strand of barbed wire to make her passage less difficult. Then he continued on, following some trail clear only to himself. She could see the routes the cows took along the fence line. She followed until he stopped and then glanced past him at the knee-high yellowing grass. The parallel tracks of a small vehicle were clear even to her.

"What the heck is that?" she said.

"ATV. Came from up there where the fence

was cut. Saw the tracks this morning, but with the shooting, it slipped my mind until you showed up in my driveway. He rode down this way, in a circle, gathering your herd. Cattle tracked that way." He pointed.

"He?" she said.

"Could be a she. Won't know unless they get out of the vehicle."

They walked a bit farther on. The grass was flat by the fence. She could imagine her cattle pressed up against the barbed wire.

"Stopped here and then headed that way." He pointed back the way the vehicle had come.

"What was it doing on my land?" She had a sick feeling in her stomach as she looked at the grass flattened on both sides of the fence line. They'd exited there. But how?

Clay advanced to the fence and touched one of the wires. It fell, snagging the one below it and bringing that down, as well. Clay pointed to the splice, where someone had reconnected the cut line exactly beside one of the barbs using thin pieces of wire.

"You've been rustled," said Clay.

"But they didn't steal them."

"No. Just drove them to the road and called the livestock manager so we'd come scoop up your cows."

"Who made the call?"

"Don't know. But you best ask and take a few photos of this. You got a phone that does that?"

She shook her head. Clay withdrew an older model smartphone and began photographing the line and the break and the one remaining patch. Then he photographed the pasture and, for good measure, took a short movie.

"That should do it."

"I'm calling the cops again," she muttered.

"Let's check up top first."

She nodded glumly. Then realized something and stopped.

"I can get my cows back. If someone cut the fences and drove them out, I shouldn't have to pay the fine."

"If you can prove it."

"You just did."

Now he looked glum.

"What's wrong?"

"Nothing," he said, continuing back the way they came, exiting through the broken fence and replacing the small bits of wire.

"Why didn't they fix the upper one?" she asked pausing as Clay took more photos.

Clay tucked away his camera. "Don't know. Maybe they ran out of time or someone saw them. Where were you this morning?"

Chapter Four

Izzie stilled at Clay's accusation as heat flooded her face. Indignation rose with the pitch of her voice.

"You think I did this?"

"What? No! I just asked where you were."

Now her face flamed with embarrassment.

"I don't accuse folks of things, Izzie. That's Gabe's job."

She touched his arm and felt his bicep flex beneath the worn cotton. "I'm sorry."

He nodded his acceptance.

"I was with the ferrier. Biscuit and the other horses were getting their feet trimmed and teeth filed."

"So the ferrier was here. I wonder who else knew you'd be with him."

She started to compile a list in her mind. When she got to ten people she sighed and gave up. Clay trailed back out on to the road. Izzie went to her truck to grab some wire to fix the gaping hole.

"I wouldn't do that until after they have a look. The police, I mean."

Izzie wasn't leaving a hole between two posts, so Clay helped her rig a temporary closure.

When they got back to the truck Clay got her door again. After she climbed up into the cab, he hesitated before closing the door.

"Somebody is after your herd, Izzie. You need to watch your back."

Izzie met the concern in his gaze and tried to look brave. But inside her fears gobbled her up. Keeping the herd was hard. Keeping them while under attack…

She reached out and Clay took her hand. He gave a squeeze.

"Thank you for helping me."

He flushed and released her, stepping back, closing the door. She watched him round the front of her truck.

She started the engine and waited as he climbed in. She was so darn lucky that he was a big enough man to put aside her snub and help her when she really needed him. Would she have done the same?

Izzie swallowed her uncertainty as these questions made her shift with discomfort.

The motor idled, and Clay glanced her way, his hat in his hands and brows raised in an unspoken question.

"I don't know what I would have done if you didn't agree to help me."

His voice was quiet. Intimate. "I'll always help you, Izzie."

"Maybe we can be friends again."

His brows lifted higher. "Is that what we are?"

Was he thinking of what she had been? How could you ever be friends after you loved someone? Was it even possible to mend the fences cut between them?

"We could be," she whispered.

Clay faced forward and said nothing as she drove them up the hill.

"There is cell service at the top of the mountain here. I can call the police from up there." She hoped the gunmen and the police were gone. Really, she wanted nothing more than to wake up and find this day was all a nightmare. But then she looked at Clay sitting beside her again and wondered if it was all worth it just for these few minutes together.

At the top of the pasture, she turned onto the improved road. The sun shone through the tall pines to the west in flashing bands of brilliance, but it was starting to go down now. Clay directed her where to park and then exited the truck. Izzie followed, just as she always had. What would he do if he knew the reason she'd dated Martin? Would he be flattered or angry?

It had been a stupid, childish idea, and it had blown up in her face.

The entire episode was embarrassing. Funny that Martin had charmed her mother into believing he was a good guy. A good Christian boy, Carol Nosie had called him. He'd fooled a lot of folks with his manners. But she'd known what he was, and she'd still agreed to go out with him, for a while.

She could see nothing on the gravel that Clay studied, so she watched him, enjoying the way the light gilded his skin and the stretch of denim and cotton as he stooped and rose.

On the gravel road the rocks crunched beneath his feet. He walked slowly, his eyes scanning back and forth. At last they reached the wide bulldozed stretch that had been muddy the last time she'd been up here but now was packed earth. Clay made a sound in his throat, and Izzie wanted to ask him what he saw, but she cultivated patience. He walked back and forth, ventured into the woods, knelt a few times, lifted a stone, and examined a branch. The only thing Izzie saw for sure were the prints of her cattle that had made it up this far. She tried to count the number of cows, but they circled back on themselves, so she gave up.

"Look," she said, finding an interesting track at the edge of a drying puddle. "Dog."

"Coyote," he said from some forty feet off.

She gripped her rifle tight as she squatted to examine the print. Why hadn't she learned to track?

"This way," Clay said, and she followed him past the cut of dirt, up the steep incline sprinkled with quaking aspen. She glanced up at sunlight shining its last rays on the golden leaves and smiled at the beauty. With her focus elsewhere, she did not see Clay stop and nearly ran right into him. He stood with hands on hips, staring down. She heard the buzz of many flies before her attention snapped to the three cows all lying motionless in the tall grass. Her cows.

Izzie gave a little cry and tried to rush past him. But he halted her with one hand, effortlessly bringing her back to his side.

"That your brand?" he asked.

She glanced at the flank of the closest cow and recognized the two interlocking circles.

"Yes. Are they dead?"

The question was answered by their absolute stillness. It was two heifers and one yearling. Their legs stuck out straight as if they had been stuffed and then toppled, and their eyes were a ghostly white. Izzie calculated her herd. One hundred and eleven in all, minus one to Clay, minus three to death was a hundred and eight. But that included the fifty-one now impounded.

She glanced around, searching for more dead cows. This was a disaster.

She threw up her hands in frustration. "What are they doing way up here?"

"You got a fence between this and the upper pasture?"

"Too much ground to cover. They mostly just stay together in the pasture."

Clay pointed at the grass. "Coyotes chased them."

Izzie fumed and lifted her rifle to her shoulder, searching for the coyotes. Then her brain re-engaged, and she realized coyotes couldn't take down two heifers. They'd been after the yearling.

Clay rested a hand on her shoulder and gave a squeeze before releasing her. She turned from her dead cattle to glance up at him.

"Coyotes didn't do that! There's not a mark on them."

He nodded his head and glanced back at the carcasses. Flies buzzed and landed in their nostrils and on their filmy white eyes. She looked at the lolling tongues and noted the saliva was a neon-green color. She'd never seen anything like it before.

"What's that?" she asked, her voice a whisper.

He shook his head. "Not sure. Sick?"

The very thought of that caused a surge of terror to crash through her like a wave, the impact rocking her on her feet. Clay steadied her with a gentle clasping of her elbow. She shook him off, looking for a fight.

"My cows aren't sick!" she said, more to herself than to him. She could think of no greater catastrophe than sick cows. But her eyes locked on the green sputum. Oh, Lord help her if they had something contagious. The tribe would order them slaughtered. She'd be left with nothing. And without the cattle, she couldn't maintain the permits. She gripped the rifle tight and tried to think.

Clay withdrew his phone from his front pocket.

She clasped his wrist, feeling the cool skin and the roping tendons beneath.

"Wait a minute."

He did, but his face was granite.

"Give me a second." She glanced around as if someone would come to her rescue. But no one ever did that. She stared up at Clay. "Someone chased my herd onto the road. Now they are trying to make it look like my cattle are sick. It's another setup."

"Maybe. Need a vet to know for sure."

She gripped the forearm of the hand that held the phone.

"Don't call them," she begged.

His eyes widened, and his mouth gaped. Then his look went cold and his posture still. Her cheeks burned with shame. Had she just asked him to break the law?

He lifted his arm, and she let her numb fingers slip from his sleeve as the shame burned her up with the last of the sunlight.

Clay drew up a number and pressed the call button. A moment later she heard a familiar voice. "Gabe? It's Clay. I've got a problem."

Chapter Five

Clay and Kino had gone over the tracks using floodlights. Kino agreed with what Clay saw. Gabe was busy directing the investigation, but he took a look at some of the more important signs. All the Cosen boys had learned to read sign from both their father and from their maternal grandfather. Reading sign was a part of their inheritance and the skill that had made their ancestors so valuable to the US Cavalry. And Clay's ancestors had found Geronimo. It was why their tribe was still on their ancestral land, an anomaly for most Native peoples.

Some things never changed because now Apache trackers were in demand with Border Patrol, Immigration and Customs and, lately, the US military. Clyne had spent six months as a special instructor in Afghanistan teaching elite military units how to track terrorists in the desert. And Clay and Kino had only just returned from the

Sonora Desert, where they had tracked drug traffickers entering over the Mexican border.

Clay was cold, hungry and surly by the time Gabe got the go-ahead to call the Office of the State Veterinarian, from tribal officer Arnold Tessay. Clearly, Izzie had forgotten her offer to buy him dinner. Right now, he could eat that frozen pizza cold.

Both Tessay and Clyne arrived well past dark. The tribe's president was in Washington testifying before the House of Representatives on Indian Affairs. Gabe also had called Donner, since he managed the tribal livestock and needed to be made aware that there might be some new illness killing cows on the Rez. Gabe told Clay that Donner was calling both Pizarro, who covered the tribe's cattle business, and Soto, who oversaw livestock health. Donner and Pizarro arrived together. Clay knew from his boss's angry stride that he was pissed. He was a big man, nearly as tall as Clay, though twenty years and forty pounds separated them. His face was fleshy and had been pulled by time and gravity. Behind him came Boone Pizarro. By contrast, Pizarro's skin stretched tight as a drumhead over his angular face, and his body was thin with ropy muscles. Clay heard that his wife preferred the casinos to cooking, but whatever the reason, Pizarro had a perpetual hungry look. Both men stopped before him, expressions stern.

"I don't remember sending you over here again," Donner said to Clay.

"No, sir. Ms. Nosie asked me to check for sign. Her herd didn't break loose. The fences were cut."

Pizarro's mouth went thin. "Cutting is a serious charge."

Thankfully Gabe stepped up at that moment. "They were cut, all right."

"And you didn't see this earlier?" said Donner.

Izzie interjected now. "Maybe it was the bullets that distracted him, or being pulled in for questioning."

Donner cast her a sour look. While Pizarro laughed, Clay gave her a slow shake of his head. He didn't need that kind of help. His boss was angry enough. Plus sarcasm might not be the best option against a man who had the authority to quarantine her entire herd. Beside him, Izzie fumed but said no more.

"You got any suspects?" Pizarro asked Gabe.

Tessay moved closer to Clyne, making Izzie the lone woman in a circle of men. She always had been, he realized, as a rancher and before that with her two brothers and father. But Clay noticed they'd closed Izzie out. He stepped back, and she wedged in beside him.

"Nope," said Gabe, his posture relaxed. "Just starting the investigation."

If he was stressed by the late hour or the presence of his superiors from the tribal council, he gave no sign and instead only radiated confidence and authority. Clay admired that. Gabe was a keen observer of everything, and he was very good at noticing inconsistencies. Perhaps that was why he went into law enforcement. Or it could have been to make up for their father. That was a tough legacy.

Gabe hitched a thumb in his utility belt, as comfortable with his sidearm as Clay was uncomfortable with one.

"We got shots fired, cut fences, repaired fences intended, I believe, to give the illusion of an intact fence. We've also got three dead cows with no sign of predation."

"Disease?" asked Tessay.

"Vets will tell us that. They're en route."

Pizarro and Donner exchanged looks.

"Where's Soto?" asked Pizarro. "He should be here."

"On his way," said Gabe, failing to be sidetracked. "Either of you have any idea why this area has been improved?" Gabe directed his attention to his brother Clyne and Arnold Tessay. As tribal leaders, they were the logical ones to ask.

"Not me," said Clyne.

Tessay hesitated and then shook his head. "Don't know."

"Looks like a pretty nice level area. Not sure why it's here," said Gabe.

His comment went without reply from any of those gathered, but Izzie was shifting from side to side. Did she know more than she had told him? Clay watched Gabe's attention flick to Izzie, and Clay resisted the urge to still her nervous motion.

"We need to quarantine Nosie's herd," said Pizarro.

"I don't want to get folks all in a tizzy over nothing," said Tessay.

"We don't know what killed those cows, yet," said Gabe. "But better safe than sorry."

Donner looked to Clay. "Pick them up in the morning. I've got no budget for overtime."

"You can't just take my cows," said Izzie, but her voice lacked confidence, for she surely knew that they could and would do just that. Keeping all cattle certified and disease free was essential to their survival.

Clyne rested a hand on Izzie's shoulder. It was a fatherly gesture, and still it raised the hackles on Clay's neck. He had to resist the urge to shove his brother as if they were still kids. Not that he'd ever won a fight against his eldest brother. Clyne was eight years his senior. Clay thought he might just be able to take him now. Instead he reined himself in.

"Izzie, we'll expedite this. I promise. If possible, we'll get your cows a clean bill of health and get the ones that were impounded returned to you as soon as we can. But you have to help us here."

"Councilman," said Izzie, "my family depends on our herd."

"She's no different than the rest of us in that," said Tessay, whom Clay recalled had a cow or two pastured in the tribe's communal herd.

"She is different," argued Clay, wondering when he'd suddenly decided to pursue a career in public speaking. "Because she has more cattle than most of the other members of the tribe and because her family has been herding on this land since before they built Pinyon Fort."

Gabe was rubbing the back of his neck in discomfort. Clay wondered if he were the one causing that pain. He glanced to Clyne to find him grinning at him like a fool. Izzie gaped at him as if he had just sprouted a crown like one of the mountain spirits.

Donner grasped Clay's arm. "Will you excuse us for a minute?"

Clay had a sinking feeling he was about to get fired as his boss led him out of earshot. Donner stopped them a short distance from the others.

"That's my boss you're dressing down," he said.

Clay stared at the ground. Outside of the circle of the headlights, there wasn't much to see.

"I'm sorry, sir."

"What's gotten into you? I mean, what does it matter to you, anyway?"

"Nothing," Clay admitted. "Izzie is an old friend."

Donner snorted. "Friend, huh?"

Izzie had stopped being his concern long ago. She'd made it very clear that she didn't want any part of him...until today, or was it yesterday? He glanced at the sky, glittering with stars, and decided from the angle of Orion that it was past midnight. He stretched his shoulders.

"You working for her?"

"No. Well, she asked me to read sign."

His boss flapped his arms. "It's called moonlighting, and I can fire you for it. You can't work for someone else while you're working for me."

"I—I didn't know," Clay said.

Donner made a face. "I believe you, son. But this isn't just about what's right and wrong. It's about the appearance of right and wrong. Appearance is the same as reality."

Clay scratched the stubble on his chin. "I'm interested in the truth."

"Son, an inspector working for a rancher is a conflict of interest. That didn't occur to you?"

It had. In fact he'd warned Izzie that he would not be a part of anything illegal.

"I just read the signs."

"Okay. You read the signs. It's done. I'm giving you a warning and telling you to stay out of it. She needs help, she can hire your kid brother to track. Anyone on the Rez but you."

"Yes, sir."

"You know I went to school with your father?"

Clay did know because his uncle Luke had told him when he'd spoken to Donner about hiring Clay. His uncle Luke Forrest was his father's half brother and so was not a Cosen.

"And your uncle put in a word for you. So do us both a favor. Keep out of politics. When Tessay or Clyne are talking, you hush up unless you need to say, 'Yes, sir.' You got that?"

"Yes, sir." He said it without sarcasm but still gleaned a long, hard stare.

His boss left him standing there and returned to the circle. Clay swiped his hand at the long grass in frustration. Izzie needed his help. But he sure needed this job. Kino found him first.

"They're wrapping it up for tonight. Can't see anything, anyway."

"The vet here?"

"Yeah. And Soto finally made it. They're gonna set up tents and do the necropsy right here.

Damn, that green puss is something. Ever seen anything like it?"

Clay gave his head a slow shake. "How long for results?"

"Couple days, at least." Kino rested his hands on his hips, tucking his thumbs under the utility belt and staring out at the investigation, winding down as men headed for their vehicles.

"What?" said Clay. He knew his brother well enough to know that he wasn't done talking.

Kino shrugged. "Clyne is worried about you and Izzie."

"What about us?"

"None of my business. His, either. I told him that. But you took it pretty hard the last time is all."

When she'd dumped him. Great, now his brothers where discussing his love life. Add it to the long list of his failures. Must make a nice change from gossiping about his other shortcomings.

"She hired me to read sign."

"Okay. Just be careful."

Did Kino mean because of the shooting or because he'd been a complete train wreck when Izzie had broken it off?

"Yeah. I'll tell her to ask you if she needs any more help reading sign." He called himself a liar even as he uttered the words. "Told her all I could. That should be that." But he hoped it wasn't. He wanted to see her again, was already plotting how he could make that happen. She owed him dinner.

"Good, because Gabe told me to remind you to leave the police work to us." He kept his head down now as he delivered his message.

Clay tore off his hat and raked his fingers through his hair.

"Sorry," muttered Kino.

Clay turned his back on Kino and headed toward the group of men. He noted that Izzie's truck was already gone. What had he expected, a goodnight kiss?

Clay glanced down out of habit, scanning the ground, and saw something he hadn't before. A track—a big one, one that did not belong up here in the middle of nowhere.

Clay lifted his head. He had to find Gabe.

Chapter Six

Izzie did not sleep well or much. Her wake-up call the next morning was Gabe Cosen serving her with notice that the remainder of her cows would be seized and quarantined. Her mother returned from running errands and confronted her about seeing "that Cosen boy again." Her mother loved gossip, unless she or her family were the subject of talk. Izzie wondered if her mother ever tired of being above reproach.

"Of all the people in this tribe to call. Really, Isabella. What were you thinking? What about that nice Mr. Patch? He certainly has made his interest known. And he has all that cattle."

Izzie cringed, and her mother's hands went to her hips.

"What's wrong with him? I mean, we could certainly use some help around here."

"We're doing fine." At least they had been yesterday. Now she felt as if the ground beneath her was sliding away.

"I mean, Clay Cosen, do you honestly want our name and his linked? Your father certainly didn't."

The below-the-belt blow hit home. Izzie flinched. It had been her father's opposition that had finally gotten her to break it off with Clay. She'd been so sure her parents would change their minds about Clay, and then he had been arrested. Case closed. Her mother had basked in smug satisfaction at being right again while her father had offered comfort. How she missed her father, still, every single day.

"I don't want that man on my land again," she said to Izzie.

Izzie wanted to tell her mother that the land did not belong to them, but to the tribe. They had use of it by permit only. She wanted to tell her mother that she was a grown woman who could see who she liked, and she wanted to tell her mother that running the ranch was not her business because her husband had left that job to Izzie. Instead she said, "I've got chores."

"But wait. I want to hear what is going on up there."

Izzie kept going, knowing that her mother didn't want anything badly enough to walk into a pasture dotted with cow pies and buzzing with flies. Izzie changed direction and headed for her pickup, deciding that would be faster than riding Biscuit.

"He's trouble," her mother called after her.

Izzie swung up behind the wheel. "Mom, I've got bigger trouble right now than Clay Cosen." So why was she thinking of him instead of how to get back her cows? "I just got notice. They're taking the rest of the herd, Mom."

Carol pressed a hand to her chest. "But why?"

"Quarantined."

"But…you… They… Isabella Nosie, you have to get them back."

Finally, something on which they agreed.

"Working on it." She pulled the truck door closed and started the engine, using the wipers to move the dust that blanketed her windshield.

Izzie headed up to the area where Clay had found the dead cows and now saw that a large white tent had been erected over the spot. Several pickups were parked beside the police cars in the gravel pad. Only one was familiar. It belonged to her neighbor Floyd Patch.

Izzie groaned as Floyd headed straight toward her. His gait was rushed, almost a jog. His skinny legs carried his round body along, reminding Izzie of a running ostrich. He was short, prematurely gray, with bulging eyes and skin that shone as if it had been recently waxed. His usual smile had been replaced by a look that hovered between stormy and category-five tornado.

She didn't even have the driver's-side door shut when he was on her like a hungry flea on a hound. He hitched his fists against his narrow hips and drew himself up, making his shirt draw tight across his paunch. It was hard for Izzie to recall that she'd initially found his attentions flattering. Now she greeted his occasional appearances with the reluctant resignation of an oncoming headache.

"I don't appreciate you sending the police to my door," said Floyd, his voice higher than usual.

"I did no such thing."

"Asking me where I was yesterday and checking the tires of my truck, as if I'm some kind of criminal. They ought to check Clay Cosen's tires. I heard he was up here yesterday. What did you tell them, that I poisoned your cattle?"

"No, I never—"

"And I have to find out from the police that you've got cows dying up here."

"Floyd, it only just happened."

"Yesterday. And you didn't think I might want to know? I've got my own herd to protect." He pointed in the direction of his pastures, across the road and down the hill. His pasture was rocky and more wooded, because her ancestors had invested more sweat in clearing the land.

"There's been no contact between your cattle and mine, and you haven't been on my property in two weeks or more. Your herd is in no danger."

Floyd's gaze flicked away, and he pursed his lips. *Had he been on her land?*

His gaze swung back to hers. "If there is no danger, then why did they quarantine your herd?"

"A precaution."

"I understand that one of your dead cows had green stuff in its mouth. That's not normal."

If Floyd knew that, then everyone else did. "Who told you that?"

He didn't answer, just continued on. "What if it gets in the water? What if it's airborne? Three cows don't just drop. Something killed them."

"Floyd, I have to go," she said.

The day just got worse from there. Izzie spent the afternoon waiting for information outside the necropsy tent of the State Office of Veterinarian Services. By day's end, she knew only that the cows had showed renal and liver damage, mucus in the lungs and swelling in their brains. Cause of death was ruled as sudden cardiac arrest in all three. As to why, well, that was the question. What was it, and was it contagious?

The best answer she received was that more tests were needed. On the way back to her truck, Izzie found Chief Gabe Cosen speaking to Clay, who was sweat-stained, saddle-worn and sexy as hell. Clay noticed her approach and gave her a sad smile.

"Didn't think you'd be back up here," she said to Clay. "After your boss warned you off."

Chief Gabe Cosen quirked his brow at her. Clay's brother was handsome with classic good looks and that distinctive angular jaw shared by all the Cosen brothers. But it was only Clay who made her heart pound.

"I was just telling Clay that I'd served you notice to collect the rest of your herd. I'm sorry, Izzie."

She pressed her lips together to resist the temptation of tears.

"And he told me that you hired him to have a look around yesterday."

Of course Clay told his brother. Did she really expect him to pick her needs over his brother's investigation?

"I'm looking into who cut your fences. Sorry for your troubles." Gabe tipped his hat, the gray Stetson the tribal police wore in the cold season. He turned to Clay. "Well, I've got to verify what you found." With that the chief of police made a hasty retreat.

"What did you find?"

"I wanted to tell you yesterday, but you'd gone when I got back here, and I didn't think you wanted me knocking on your front door."

That made her flush.

"Was I wrong about that?"

Izzie thought of her mother's earlier tizzy and shook her head. She let her shoulders slump. She lived for the day that her brothers were old enough to take over, and she could live her own life. But from the way it looked now, there would be nothing to pass along to them. Izzie rallied. She could not let that happen. No one and nothing would stop her from retrieving every last cow.

"I've got to get them back," she said.

Clay motioned to her truck and lowered the back gate. Then he offered her a hand up. They sat side by side amid the comings and goings of inspectors, livestock managers, tribal council. More than one cast them a cursory glance, and she wondered which ones would be reporting to their wives, who would report to her mother later on. Her mother had connections like the roots of an ancient pinyon pine. They were branched and deep.

"It looks like the rodeo," Izzie muttered.

"Yeah." Clay surveyed their surroundings and then focused on her. "Izzie, you hired me to give you a report."

"I can't pay you now." She lowered her head, fighting against the burning in her throat. Crying in front of Clay was too humiliating, so she cleared her throat and gritted her teeth until the constriction eased.

Clay placed a hand on her shoulder and squeezed. She glanced up, eyes somehow still dry.

"Izzie, you had a heck of a big truck up here. Only left yesterday."

"You mean the earth-moving machinery, bull-dozer and dump trucks?"

"No, I mean an eighteen-wheeler, actually, two of them."

"Eighteen-wheelers? Yesterday. Eighteen-wheelers can't haul dirt."

"That's right. But they were here. And they were loading and unloading the trucks. Moving contents from one to another. Five guys."

"What were they doing up here?"

"Not certain."

She knew that look. He had suspicions.

"What, Clay?"

"Moonshining, maybe, or drugs."

"You mean stashing drugs here?" She glanced around, half expecting to see a pile of boxes. She'd heard about the Mexican cartels using Rez land for holding their illegal merchandise, guns, drugs and people because treaty restrictions pre-vented federal authorities from entering sacred lands and from conducting investigations with-out obtaining permission first.

"But that wouldn't kill my cows."

"It might. If they were cooking up here."

"Cooking what?"

"Crystal meth."

Izzie rocked backward as confusion wrinkled her brow.

"I don't understand."

"There are fumes, by-products. They are poisonous."

"Poisonous?"

"Gabe is checking for residue."

Izzie straightened as a ray of light broke through the clouds. If Clay was right, then there was nothing wrong with her herd. She could get them back. She could still keep her promise to her father.

"They're not sick!" Izzie threw herself into Clay's arms. "Oh, thank you!"

He stiffened for just a moment, and then he wrapped his arms around her. She didn't know how it happened. She was pressed against him as relief flooded through her, replaced a moment later with blinding white heat. Her body tingled. She tipped her head back, offering Clay her mouth. He did not hesitate but swooped down, angling his head as he kissed her greedily. Her fingers raked his back as she hovered between the sweetness of the contact of their mouths and the need for so much more.

"Isabella Mary Nosie!"

Izzie recognized her mother's sharp admonition and pushed off Clay's chest at the same moment he released her. The result was that she rocked dangerously on the tailgate, and only Clay's quick reflexes kept her from toppling to the ground. He freed her arm the moment she regained her equilibrium and slid to his feet.

Izzie faced her mother, who stood with eyes blazing with fury as she glared at her eldest daughter. Izzie tried to keep her head up, but she found herself shrinking under her mother's censure and the curious stares of the men she had forgotten were even there.

"What do you think you are doing?" asked her mother.

Clay looked to her, but all she could do was stammer, so he answered instead.

"Izzie asked me to help her figure out what happened to her cows."

Her mother shot her a look, and Izzie nodded.

"Well, that's a fine how-do-you-do." She turned to Izzie. "He's a felon. You don't ask felons to do police work."

Izzie found her tongue. "He's not a felon."

Her mother laughed. "Criminal, then. A skunk can't change his stripe, and this one is just like his father. Now you come along home with me this instant. If word of this gets out, I'll die of shame."

Izzie straightened her spine. "No, Mom. I can't. I've got work to do."

Her mother gasped and then glared, but Izzie held her ground, drawing a gentle strength from Clay, who stood silent by her side.

"Work? Is that what you call it? You said you were up here to get our cattle back. Instead I find you fiddling with this…trash."

Beside her, Clay showed no sign that the insult had landed. He remained still and relaxed, propped against the back of her truck.

"Go home, Mom."

"I don't like it," she said at last and wheeled away in the direction she had come.

Izzie sagged against the tailgate, feeling suddenly like a kite that had lost the buoyant wind.

"What did I just do?" she whispered.

Clay's mouth quirked. "You stood up to your mother."

Chapter Seven

Despite Clay's theory about the possibility of illegal drug activity, Clay's boss had received orders from Franklin Soto to collect and quarantine
Izzie's herd until such time as they were shown to
be disease-free. So late Wednesday morning Clay
rode beside Mr. Donner in the big cattle truck toward Izzie's place, followed by a pickup with two
more cowboys pulling a four-horse trailer. His
boss had an ATV for herding, which was now in
the back of the pickup.

Donner had called Izzie before their arrival to
inform her that her herd would be collected today.
They were working with the tribal livestock coordinator, who currently rode behind them in his
pickup with the tribal council member Arnold
Tessay. Mr. Pizarro managed grazing permits for
the tribe and wanted a look at the area that was
causing all the fuss in full daylight, so Tessay had
agreed to ride him up there.

Back in Black Mountain, Franklin Soto, the

tribe's livestock inspector, was waiting to take custody of her herd.

Clay fiddled with his lariat, dreading the task of rounding up the rest of Izzie's cattle.

"You remember me telling you that reality is less important than perception," said Donner.

"Yes, sir."

"Well, you kissing Isabella Nosie before God and everyone has put me in a tight spot."

"I'm sorry, sir."

"You stay away from that gal or folks will assume that her special favors to you are getting her special treatment from us."

Clay's jaw clenched as he considered the gossip he might have started by kissing Izzie. It had all happened so fast, and he hadn't thought. He needed to think. Not thinking, taking things as they came. It had all gotten him into trouble. He didn't want that again.

"...ruin her reputation and call into question every blasted decision that I make all in one... You hearing me, son?"

Clay collected his wandering thoughts and nodded as his fist tightened on the stiff coils of rope. He never meant to hurt Izzie, but his boss saying that kissing him would ruin her reputation didn't sit well, even if it were true. So he said nothing, because he needed this job and wasn't likely to get another.

His boss knew his way around cows and also politics. Donner had kept his job by staying neutral in contentious issues and staying out of controversial decisions. But if you asked him, he'd only say that he didn't set tribal policy, he just enforced it.

"Did you know that your uncle Luke and I were teammates?"

Played basketball together, Clay knew.

Donner continued. "He assured me that you'd do the job and not cause me a lick of trouble." Donner glanced at him for a long moment before returning his attention to the road. "You've caused me more than a lick already."

Clay stilled, waiting to hear that he'd be fired.

"I'm real sorry, sir. It won't happen again."

"Your actions reflect on you and your family, Clay. Now they also reflect on me. You should know that by now."

He sure did. Clyne was a tribal council member. Gabe was chief of police. Even his younger brother was a patrolman. While Clay's claim to fame was spending eighteen months in a juvenile detention center and six months looking for work before his uncle intervened. Why had Donner said yes?

Donner had accepted his uncle Luke's request to hire Clay when no one else would. Now Clay wondered if his boss had acted to help an old

friend or to curry favor from an up-and-coming
FBI officer and war hero.

Clay's uncle was everything Clay was not. He
had a clean record, no skeletons in his closet.
He'd distinguished himself in Afghanistan and
was recruited into the FBI. He had prestige, position, influence, power and the respect of everyone on the Rez.

Clay wondered again if it was possible to regain what he had lost that night on Highway 4.

He'd made a mistake. But would he be forever
marked by that error like a cow after contact with
a hot branding iron?

Clay thought it might be different after he'd
come back from the Shadow Wolves. Being a
member of that elite tracking unit of Immigration
and Customs Enforcement carried some serious
distinction. But not for Clay. Things here were
the same as always, and folks just assumed that
Clyne or Uncle Luke or Gabe had asked someone else to throw Clay a bone.

He watched the pastures roll along. This was
Floyd Patch's grazing area. Rocky with clumps
of woods and farther from the stream that cut
through Izzie's property. Floyd had to dig a well
for water.

"One more thing, son."

He turned his attention back to Donner.

"If you are right about the activity up top, well, Izzie might be involved."

He blinked in stunned surprise. When he found his voice it was to issue a denial. "She's not."

"How do you know?"

He didn't of course. But he did know Izzie. "She's never been involved with that sort of thing. Never."

"Well, here's something to chew on—her mother once had a gambling problem, which is why her dad left her."

Clay didn't know Izzie's dad had ever left her mom.

"Then she found God and blah, blah, they got it worked out. But he left the herd to Izzie. Too much for one little gal, my opinion, but that's not my business. Word is that her mom's got some unpaid debts. People with financial trouble can make some bad choices."

Clay sank back into the seat. Was it possible? Was Izzie's mom still a gambler? Did Izzie have unpaid debts? Clay didn't want to believe it, but he'd learned from hard experience that things were not always what they seemed.

"Don't hitch your wagon to that horse, son. Right now, Izzie is in trouble, and she *is* trouble. Best keep your distance."

When a friend was in trouble, wasn't that when they needed you? Clay remembered when everyone he counted on had left him. But not his family. They had stuck.

A tribal police car passed them, pulling in front of their truck and leading them the rest of the way to the Nosie place.

Donner turned the wheel with a grunt, and they headed up Izzie's drive. They passed a police unit parked by the fence. Pizarro pulled beside it, and Donner stopped in the drive.

Izzie stood before the gate. She had all the cattle in the lower pasture and waited by the fence, her face stoic and her posture erect. Clay's heart hitched at the sight of her, alone with only one hired hand, Max Reyes, to help her. Must have taken them all morning to round them up.

"Any results on the blood work on her cows?" asked Clay.

"That's between your brother, Gabe and the state. We just do as we're told."

"Yes, sir."

"Come on. Jeez, I hate this part."

He'd expected to see Gabe there, but it was Kino waiting in the squad car. He stepped out as Donner descended. Clay hung back with Kino as Donner and Izzie exchanged a few words. Donner handed over the order of collection.

He and the other two boys got to work. They didn't need the horses or ATV. Just used their lariats to shoo the herd to the truck. Clay drove the first load in with his coworker, Roger To-lino, riding shotgun. Once they had them in the tribal quarantine area, they returned for the second load.

Izzie clutched the order of removal in her hand like a stress ball, watching in silence as they gathered her remaining cows. Beside her, her mother smoked a cigarette and focused her attention on Clay and the distance he kept from Izzie.

Clay had never seen Izzie look more downcast, not even after Martin's death. Then, at least, she had wept. Now she stared like a woman in shock. He wanted to go to her, comfort her. The urge to do so was strong and unrelenting.

But he couldn't.

Still his eyes found her often. Izzie did not look at him. She had her attention only on her disappearing herd.

Gabe arrived, and he and Kino spoke by the fence. His brothers did not help or speak to him as he did his job and they did theirs. Clay and the others went to work loading up the remaining eighteen-odd cows. But before Clay climbed back in the cab, Gabe pulled him aside.

"Grandma is worried about you," he said.

"I'm all right." But he wasn't. His heart hurt for Izzie, and he felt as he had after the trial when the records were sealed because of his age. It would be better, they all said. But it wasn't. In the vacuum of knowledge, folks had just made up their own stories, theories, speculation. Most were worse than what had actually happened. At least in the versions he had heard, he didn't come out looking like a damned fool.

Which was worse—to look a criminal or a fool?

They'd be doing the same to Izzie soon. Her name would be linked either to drug activity on her land or bovine sickness. Which was worse?

The girl with the sterling reputation was about to take her first trip through the mud.

Clay should find some satisfaction in that. His reputation was the reason she'd cited for breaking them up. But Martin had had her parents snowed. They'd believed he was a gentleman. He hadn't been. Still, you didn't speak badly about the dead.

Gabe cleared his throat, and Clay returned his attention to his brother.

"Grandma says she wants you to come to supper tonight."

"All right."

Gabe turned to go, and Clay reached out, clasping his elbow, drawing him back.

"Any results from the state?"

Gabe glanced around as if seeing who might overhear. Then he walked away without a word.

But Kino lingered, then spoke. "Asphyxiation," Kino said. "No blood work yet."

"Mechanical or...?"

"Clay, it's an ongoing investigation. Okay?"

Kino gave him a pained look as Gabe, now Kino's boss, retraced his steps, coming to a stop beside Kino.

"Her cows aren't sick, are they?" asked Clay.

Gabe adjusted his felt hat so the brim shaded his eyes that now glittered like a hawk's. "Stay out of it, Clay," said Gabe. "It's bad business."

Chapter Eight

Izzie waited in her pickup outside the offices of the tribal livestock manager because Clay had called. Left a message. Said it was important.

Finally Clay appeared, carrying a saddle over his shoulder as if it weighed nothing. She straightened and stared, drinking him in like a glass of cool water on a hot day. It was well past five. His clothing was dirt-smeared and dusty. He tossed his saddle in his truck and removed his work gloves.

She slid out of her pickup. At the sound of the door closing, he turned in her direction.

His brow quirked and a smile played on his lips. But it vanished by the time she reached him. He smelled of horse and sweat. Why did she find even that appealing?

Clay propped himself against the closed gate of his battered truck. He was tall and handsome, his dark eyes glittering as he looked her up and down. Did he notice that she'd changed out of her work shirt and into a gauzy peasant blouse? That her jeans were clean and her lips glossed? Izzie swallowed back her nervousness. This was about business, she reminded herself. Yet she had taken time to brush out her long hair. Now she was embarrassed that she had dressed as if going on a date. She tucked her hands in her back pockets as her heart fluttered and kept walking until she was close enough to see his long lower lashes brushing his cheeks.

"You wanted to speak to me?"

He nodded. "You look pretty."

So he noticed. She blushed.

"Want to go somewhere more private?" she asked and then thought her words sounded like an invitation she had not meant to extend.

His brow quirked again.

"I mean, so we won't be interrupted." She pressed her hand to her forehead as she made matters worse. What was wrong with her? She didn't generally trip over her own tongue. Must be the lip gloss.

Clay chuckled. "I know what you mean, Isabella. My truck or yours?"

"Mine."

"Good choice." He extended his hand, and she led the way. He scooped up his saddle and followed, dropping the gear into her truck bed. She glanced at it and then to him.

"Some things have been going missing around here."

"Ah." She reached for her door, and he beat her there, opening it for her. She could get used to this, Izzie thought, as she slipped behind the wheel. He rounded the hood, giving her time to admire his easy gait and powerful frame. The good girl after the town's bad boy. The cliché made her wince. But she'd never gotten over him or her body's reaction every time she got near him.

She pressed a hand to her flushed face as he swept up into the cab.

"The quarry?" he asked, instantly choosing the place where they had spent happier days.

"Sure."

The drive took only fifteen minutes, but it felt like forty as the silence stretched. She actually blew out a breath of relief when she put her truck in Park. They walked side by side to the water and sat on the log everyone used as a bench to watch their friends leap from the top of the quarry into the deep water below.

"Do I make you that nervous, Izzie?" he asked.

"Clay, I'm all tangled up around you."

"Because of Martin?"

And there it was, the three-hundred-pound gorilla in the room, the topic they had never spoken about.

"There is a lot about Martin and me that you don't know," she said.

"That so?"

"I thought you wanted to talk about my cattle."

"Sure. My brother tells me that the three we found up on the hill all died of asphyxiation."

"What? How do you asphyxiate a cow?"

"By removing all the oxygen from the air."

She sat back and stared out at the cliffs, the still water and then back at him. "How do you do that? Like carbon monoxide poisoning?"

"Not CO_2. Blood tests aren't back yet. But if someone was cooking crystal meth up there on your land, the gases released could kill anything that got upwind."

"How do you know that?" Izzie asked as she gave him a long assessing look.

Clay sighed and looked away, his earnest expression replaced with disappointment. "I looked it up on the internet."

"Do you think that was wise?"

He held her gaze. "I've never been wise around you, Bella."

Her lips parted, and her heart seemed to pound in her throat. She slid closer turning her attention to him. He started talking.

"The poison is called phosphine and it kills

things. Also causes visible damage to the lungs, liver and nervous system. Convulsions, coma, heart failure. And—" Clay drew a folded sheet of paper from his breast pocket "—a fluorescent green sputum."

Izzie took the sheet, scanning over the page. "Like my cows!"

She skimmed the symptoms, and he used an elegant index finger to point to the spot. There it was.

When she glanced up, it was to find Clay watching her closely. "So you didn't know?"

Izzie's brow knit, and then realization dawned and she stiffened. Briskly she folded and returned the printout. "What are you implying?"

He met her hard glare with one of his own. "I told you when you hired me that I won't be a part of anything illegal. Not even for you, Izzie. If you knew they were on your land, you best tell me right now."

Her hands fisted, and she folded her arms defensively over her chest.

"Izzie. I mean it. I've been down this road before. I will not do it again."

"Don't you trust me?"

"I don't trust anyone. Not anymore."

She sighed heavily and threw up her hands in aggravation. But she answered his question—again. "I did not know."

"Word is that you got money troubles."

She gasped. "Who told you that?"

He shrugged. Izzie looked away.

"Is it true?" His voice held a note of tenderness now.

"Yes. Mom has…some debts."

"Then they aren't your debts."

Izzie sighed. "Not technically. But someone has to pay the bills. She spends everything she can get her hands on and more."

"Gambling."

Her brow lifted. "No. Not anymore. Not since I was a kid." Izzie placed her elbows on her knees and cradled her chin in her upturned palms.

"She likes nice things." And so Izzie had shut down their line of credit at the bank. Removed her mother's name from the accounts. But the damage was done. Her mother had a nice new car, leased, and Izzie had a car payment and a six-thousand-dollar loan against her precious truck.

"And you are covering for her."

"What am I supposed to do? She's my mother."

"How?"

She lifted her chin from her hands and turned to meet his stare. "I am *not* involved with manufacturing drugs, Clay."

He nodded and looked out over the lake. "I believe you."

She didn't know if she should be insulted or

relieved. Izzie stared at the abandoned quarry as she thought about it. Finally she said, "That means a great deal to me."

He gave a humorless laugh. "It shouldn't. I'll believe just about anyone."

She cast him an odd look, and he shook his head and fell into silence. It hurt her to realize how much his past still haunted him. She wondered if she might make that a little bit better by sharing the truth.

"Clay, I want to tell you something...something about Martin."

Now Clay looked uncomfortable, his eyes shifting everywhere but back to her as his hands braced against the log, stiff and straight on either side of his body. He looked as if he were preparing to throw himself from the log and right into the lake.

"I want you to know why I went out with your friend."

He flinched, and then his mouth tipped down, making tight lines that flanked his mouth.

"Because you preferred him to me?"

"No. Because my parents would not allow me to go out with you after my cousin told them you were selling weed."

"I never..." He stopped, as if the arguing was useless.

She believed him. But after his father died,

Clay had changed, taking his anger out in rebellion. Skipping school, getting into fights. When the drunk driver killed his mother, he'd changed from rebellion to recklessness.

"You scared me back then, Clay. You were so wild. And after my aunt caught my cousin with the pot, he said you sold it to him. My parents had just gotten back together, and I didn't want any more fighting. So I said all right."

He bowed his head as the muscles at his jaw turned to granite.

"Did your cousin tell you who really supplied him with the weed?"

She shook her head.

"Martin. He supplied everyone back then."

Izzie gasped. "I didn't know that."

"He was very careful. While I…well, I was a train wreck."

"You were not."

But he had been. Back then, Clay had so much anger in him. He wouldn't tell her why, but it had begun with the trouble between his folks. Around that time, the Twin Towers fell and Clyne had joined the marines right after. Was that really fourteen years ago? Gabe, just shy of turning sixteen, had been too young to join. But Clay said he had wanted to. She knew that things had been rocky between their parents but it had taken their mom two more years before she left Clay's dad for good. Gabe, then eighteen, had found his escape riding the rodeo circuit.

That had left Clay and Kino in the middle of the mess. Clay had skipped school to go hunting, escaping into the woods. He'd failed everything and been left back, but he'd just kept cutting class. She'd reminded him that without his diploma the marines wouldn't take him. That was when he'd confessed that it killed him to come to school and have her ignore him.

Then his father had been murdered.

"I couldn't stand it," he said. "I thought you wouldn't talk to me because of my dad. He ruined a lot of things. Then he died, and I thought, finally, it will get better."

Izzie had gone to the funeral. Clay had not. But he was back in school and his grades came up. Sometimes they would study together in the school library. He'd hit the books and studied hard. He just made it through his sophomore year and she her junior year. She'd really thought he'd make it into the US Marines. Then, over the summer, his mother had gone to that competition in South Dakota. Seven months short of his seventeenth birthday...

"Then your mother and sister died. Or we thought your sister died."

He clasped his hands together and rested his forearms on his thighs. "Did I tell you that Kino is taking Lea up to South Dakota after they see some sights? He's going to find her. I just know it."

She rested a hand on his forearm. "I hope so."

He smiled and placed his hand over hers. "Iz, I was so angry at the world and myself back then, I couldn't see straight. The only good thing in all that time was you."

She resisted the pull to move closer. That had always been the way with him. She was too old now for her mother to keep her from seeing whoever she pleased. But Clay was now working for the livestock manager, who had her cows. Would they really fire him for seeing her? And hadn't she caused him enough trouble?

"I shouldn't have gone out with him. But I was so desperate to see you."

Clay gave her a look of confusion.

"Seeing Martin was the only way I could think of to be with you."

He gave his head a quick shake as if he did not believe his ears, and he gaped. She held her breath, waiting for him to call her all the things she called herself, a coward, a traitor, a child. She had been all of that and more. But he just stared, and she exhaled, realizing the next breath had to choke past the lump in her throat.

"Is that true?" he asked, his voice now a low whisper.

"Yes." Tears stung her eyes. She lifted her chin

and fought a battle against them and lost. "It was stupid. They forbade me to see you. But when I was with Martin, you were there. At least in the beginning."

"Before he started bragging."

Izzie gasped. "About us?" Shock dissipated, to be replaced with outrage. "I never once. We never! It's a lie."

He let his hand slide from hers. She returned them to her lap.

He met her gaze. Held it. Then he nodded his acceptance of her declaration. My Lord, no wonder he stayed away. And Martin had pressed her so hard.

"Did he tell you why I broke up with him?"

Clay lifted a brow. "He said he dumped you."

Izzie made a sound of frustration and swiped at the tears. Then she stared out at the blue waters where once they had all dared each other to jump from the cliffs. Clay had jumped first. Back before her parents had heard the rumors about Clay. Before they had made it impossible for her to see him. Before Clay took a gun and robbed a store.

She watched the golden sunlight of late afternoon glint on the water in wide bands. She thought that their relationship had become like that lake, just the surface visible and so many secrets hidden beneath the calm water.

Her anger burned away, leaving her hollow and more tired than she could ever remember.

"Clay, will you tell me what happened that day?"

He hesitated, then answered with his own question. "Haven't you heard the story?"

She had. Several versions. Rubin had no connections and so had gone to federal prison. Clay, the son of a drug trafficker and meth addict, had a war-hero uncle in the FBI, a brother on the tribal council and another on the police force. He'd gotten off easy. That's what folks said. But she was no longer interested in that story. She wanted *his* story.

"The paper said the records were sealed because you were a minor."

He pursed his lips and blew out a breath. "What do you want to know?"

Chapter Nine

Clay waited with a hollow resignation for the questions. In the seconds before she spoke he decided to tell her everything. Couldn't be worse than the rumors. Could it?

"Why did Rubin go to prison, when you went to a detention center?" Izzie asked. "Was it because of your uncle, like everyone says, or something else? And why did you say that you will not be set up *again*?"

He tried to think to consider his reply, but Izzie's questions buzzed about inside his head like a hive of angry hornets, stinging him. The poison of his past seeped into his bloodstream, making him as cold as the chilled lake waters.

He'd been so angry back then. Sick with anger, drowning in it. Angry at his father for getting killed and angry at Clyne for picking the marines over his miserable broken family and at Gabe for leaving to ride the rodeo circuit and then sending most of his money home. Angry at the need for that money and the way his mother watched for the mail. Angry that his older brothers found a way out that left Clay and Kino behind, at Kino for idolizing his druggie father after his death, at his mother for driving to South Dakota to win a contest only to die, and angry at the drunk driver who crossed the center line to use his pickup truck as a battering ram against his mother's Honda Civic.

All the same stuff that happened to him had happened to Gabe and Clyne, but somehow they'd never missed a step as Clyne took over providing for the family and Gabe took over managing the household. It was as if they didn't even miss them. Only Kino had faltered, fixating on his need to avenge their father, as if he deserved it, which he didn't.

"I always meant to tell you, Izzie." He cast her a glance and was immediately sorry. She glared at him. She was not the open-minded girl she had once been. Perhaps he was lucky that she even cared to ask. Or perhaps she didn't care about him so much as worrying about what kind of a man she had chosen to read sign.

"But you never did," she said.

"Hard to. I called. Left messages."

Her jaw dropped. "I didn't know that."

He sat back on the log as realization struck.

Her parents never told her. Of course they hadn't. But he had also tried in person.

"You wouldn't speak to me. I tried, that day outside Elkhorn Drugs. And again after church."

"I remember I was with my parents, who had forbidden me to speak to you. My dad threatened to turn me out if I was seen with you."

Clay dropped his head, and his blunt cut hair fell in a curtain about his face. It didn't hide his shame. Who could blame them? If Izzie had been his daughter, he wouldn't have allowed her within a mile of him.

"Clay, my father is dead, and my mom, well, she and I are having troubles. And I want to hear. Will you tell me, please? I'll listen. I promise."

It was all he could hope for.

"First, tell me what you think you know."

"All right." She looked skyward and drew in a long breath.

"I know that there was a robbery. Martin shot the clerk. The clerk was Native and a few years older than me. I didn't know him, but I know his family. Rubin was with Martin in the mini-mart. You waited in the car. Their driver. I know you took them to and from the convenience store in that car of yours."

She didn't say it was a worse piece of junk than the truck he now drove. His first car, more Bondo than metal unless you counted the coat hanger holding up the muffler. He'd been saving up then and now, for what he didn't know. A truck, a bus ticket, a fresh start, a chance to make something of himself.

Izzie gathered a strand of hair, absently sliding her fingers along the length. "I know it was a 2001 hatchback. Terrible choice for a getaway car." She arched a brow and then continued. "I know Gabe was the patrolman who came after you. I know that Martin fired at him with a pistol, and Gabe killed him with a single shot. I know it was a closed coffin. I know that you and Rubin were arrested. You went to Colorado, and Rubin went to a federal prison for four years, the maximum they could give him because the crime happened on the Rez, and Rubin is Native."

That was all so.

"You were charged with aiding and abetting and with fleeing the scene and...what else?"

"Conspiracy to commit a crime. That means they say that I knew about the planned robbery beforehand and didn't tell anyone. Anything else?"

"I know I wrote you in Colorado, and you never wrote back."

That piece of news hit him hard in the gut.

"I wrote you back," he said. "Three times. But I never got another letter."

Her gaze flicked to him. "You wrote?"

He nodded. Izzie's generous lips pressed thin. She was puzzling it out, deciding if he was lying or if her parents had taken them.

"Why should I believe you?" she asked.

"I don't know. Nobody does. Not even the courts."

Clay leaned back, gathering his knee and lacing his fingers around his shin as a counterbalance.

Izzie turned toward him, sitting sideways on the log.

"Why don't you tell me what happened?"

He felt so tired, but he faced her and gave her a look, making sure she wanted to hear. She nodded.

"Tell me." It wasn't a resounding affirmation of faith, but that needed to be earned. From what he'd seen since returning more than six years ago, not many folks were even willing to hear his side.

Izzie waited.

It was a start. But the telling was hard. He didn't like it because it made him look stupid. He had been a fool. A fool for Izzie. A fool to trust Martin. A fool to go with them that day.

"I got my GED," he said.

Her nostrils flared, and she angled her head, staring, still waiting.

"Okay, listen, okay…where to start?" His throat was dry. He shifted nervously and then thought that this just made him look guilty, as if he was thinking up a lie. He stretched his neck and rolled his shoulders as he once did before nodding at the handlers to open the shoot at the rodeo. Eight seconds on a whirlwind, that was what Clyne called riding a bucking bronc. This was worse. "That day, Rubin cut school. Martin and me, we'd already dropped out. Martin unofficially—me, well, my paperwork was submitted and filed."

Izzie shook her head in disapproval. "You were so close to graduating."

"I was miles away from graduating. I needed to get out of here. Thought if the marines wouldn't take me I could make a living riding broncs."

"Like Clyne and Gabe," she said.

But he hadn't rode broncs until after juvie.

"Anyway, Rubin's father is a trucker. He hauls different stuff." Clay didn't want to say anything that might make Izzie a target, so he kept it general. This kind of information was dangerous.

"He works for the cartels," said Izzie.

Clay raised his brows in surprise.

"That's what my father said. But he hauls regular stuff, too. Potato chips, cigarettes."

"Women," said Clay.

This time Izzie's eyes went wide.

"That day, well, Rubin said his dad had a big job, very hush-hush. Rubin thought it was weed.

It was usually weed, but when we got to his place, there was the back of the trailer in his big barn and a blue port-a-john beside it. I saw a hose leading under the closed gate of the truck, through that little opening in the back. Rubin's dad was home, but drunk, so Rubin stole his keys and opened the back. Rubin wanted to take some pot, sell it."

"But not you."

"Izzie, Clyne was home then. Recovering from the injury. Taking charge. He was on me pretty hard. He had me working for the tribal headquarters, and Gabe had just joined the force. He thought it would be a good idea to use the new dog to check my room and car for drugs."

"Good for them."

"Yeah. I was glad to have them home. Anyway, when we opened the gate it was full of women. Girls, really. Mexicans. They were so young, and they started screaming. Rubin's father came and cuffed Rubin across the mouth. Chipped a tooth in the front. He said the girls were on their way to Phoenix that night. The cartels promised them jobs as hostesses and waitresses, but they were going to end up in strip clubs and bars and massage parlors from here to Atlanta."

Izzie looked as sick as Clay felt. "What did you do?"

"I decided to tell my brother. Gabe could come

out and stop this. They were people, you know, not drugs. Kids. Younger than me, mostly. But I didn't tell that to Rubin or Martin. Martin actually asked if he could have one of them for the day."

"One of who?" Izzie's voice rang with outrage.

Clay mopped his forehead with his hand.

"A girl. He wanted one. Rubin's dad laughed and said sure, if he had two hundred dollars."

And there it was. The reason for everything that followed.

He didn't understand it because at that time Martin was still dating Izzie. Anyone who had a girlfriend as pretty and sweet and smart as Isabella Nosie didn't need to take some child. The idea of paying two hundred dollars to rape a girl made Clay sick. They hadn't looked older than thirteen.

"Then we left, and I thought it was over. But it wasn't. Martin said he wanted a pop. So I stopped at that store. I just wanted to get away from them, you know, forever. I was done. But they went in, and I didn't drive away..." God, he'd been stupid. So stupid.

"And?"

"And..." His shoulders rounded. "I had a flip phone. I used it. Called Gabe. He was new on the force then. Riding along with John Wilcox. I told him about the girls, and then I heard the shot.

Gabe heard it, too. I told him it was gunfire and where I was. Later the attorney said I knew what they were doing and just got cold feet. Rubin and Martin ran back to the car. I dropped the phone between my legs. Gabe heard most of it."

"You didn't know what they were planning beforehand?"

"That's what the judge asked and the police. Everyone. No. I didn't know."

Clay met her disbelieving stare and shook his head.

"Did you tell them all this?"

"Yes. Repeatedly."

"What did they say?"

"That I must have known or at least suspected. That was why I called Gabe. That I would have seen Martin's gun. That he would have shown off with it."

"Well?"

"He didn't. But I saw the gun when he got back in the car. I saw the money, too. A fist full of it. Martin dropped it on my car mat, and they both howled like wolves. Told me to drive and I did. Martin said he had his two hundred dollars and then some." Clay wiped his brow again, remembering.

"Are you crazy?" Clay had said. *"I can't be part of this. My brother's a cop."* And he'd just

called him and given them their location. And his phone was still connected.

"But you are a part, bro. Might even let you join the Wolf Posse. I'll talk to Randall."

The Wolf Posse was a gang, and his grandmother lived in fear that Clay would join.

"I don't want to join. I told you."

"Well, the marines don't want you."

His ears buzzed with adrenaline. What was happening? The panic welled in his chest, constricting. His mind flashed an image of the last time he felt this fear, when he had opened the door to his dad's kitchen, seeing him lying in a pool of his own blood, and his little brother Kino huddled under that kitchen table crying.

"We gotta bring the money back," *said Clay.*

"Bring it back? I just shot a guy. I'm never going back."

"You shot him? Who?" *asked Clay.*

"He got one right here." *Martin used the barrel of his gun to point at his own cheek.* "Ow. Still hot."

That's when the siren blared. Clay saw the familiar car speeding up behind them. He knew it. One just like it was parked in his grandmother's yard every night. It was either Gabe or one of the other guys on the force. There were only twelve of them. Clay slowed down.

"Are you crazy?" yelled Martin waving the gun. *"Go. Go."*

He did, running like a child from a consequence, knowing he'd never outrun this. His junker hit top speed. The wheels shimmied, and the steering went mushy. Behind him the police car gained.

"Why?" said Clay.

Martin had half turned in his seat to stare out the window at the approaching car.

"Why what?"

"Why would you do this?"

"For the money, stupid."

"The money. You shot a man for money. You lied to me for money."

"I didn't lie to you."

"Yeah? So where's the pop?" Even as he said it, Clay knew how ridiculous that sounded.

Izzie's voice jarred him from his memories.

"Is that why Rubin was charged with armed robbery and you weren't? You didn't go in?"

"Yeah. Surveillance tapes showed that Rubin drew a knife. Martin shot the clerk after he opened the register and before the guy could hit the silent alarm. Shot him in the face. He died alone on the floor behind the counter, and Martin had his money." Clay fought against the self-loathing and the urge to go back and count all the places he could have made different choices.

"Martin told me to head back to Rubin's place. I told them I had to go pick up Kino from school, which made Martin laugh."

"So you drove away?"

"He had the gun."

"The phone. Was it still on?"

"And connected. Gabe came after us. Usually the patrolmen ride alone, but Gabe was new on the force. A rookie. I kept watching for them in the rearview, and finally, there they were. Eight months on the job and here he was arresting his brother for armed robbery."

Izzie pressed her index finger to her lips and shook her head, as her eyes went wide.

"Rubin panicked and started screaming. I told Gabe I was going to hit the brakes, but Rubin thought I was talking to him and he braced against the dash.

Clay remembered that moment of perfect clarity, the moment when he realized two things simultaneously. First, he had only tolerated Martin because he couldn't stand the thought of not seeing Izzie anymore. And second, he would never again put blind trust in another person.

"I stopped. The cruiser stopped. Martin and Rubin were screaming at me. I thought I was dead. The police opened the patrol car doors, weapons drawn, and took cover. They're bulletproof, those doors."

In the rearview he had seen the driver—Gabe. "What happened then?"

"Rubin started crying. Martin called him a baby. Martin aimed the gun out the passenger window. I hit him in the ribs, but he grabbed the door handle and fell out into the road."

Clay couldn't say the rest. The guilt was too hot, choking him. He'd kept Martin from firing at his brother. But he hadn't kept Gabe from firing at Martin.

"One shot discharged by Officer Cosen," said Izzie. "That's what the newspaper said."

"One shot." *One life lost.* He should hate Martin for setting him up, using him. Instead, he felt sad and sorry and full of regrets. Martin had been so smart. He just, he just…

Izzie's hand inched closer. He didn't look at her as her hand came to rest on his shoulder and then moved to sweep his hair back from his face, tucking a strand behind his ear.

"I'm sorry," she said and rested her head on his shoulder. She nestled there, hugging his closest arm with both of hers. Not saying a word, but just sitting beside him, her presence giving comfort.

When he had won the battle over the lump in his throat and the burning in his eyes, he drew a ragged breath. Her scent, warm and appealing, rose about him with the familiar aroma of the pines. Izzie's clothing smelled like the horses she loved, but her hair smelled like sage. He lowered his head until his cheek rested on the top of hers.

"Should I have known? Should I have said I won't drive you out to Rubin's dad's? Maybe kept driving so Martin wouldn't have died there in the road."

"I don't think you could stop Martin from doing exactly as he wanted. No one could." She pressed a hand over his chest. "That's why I broke up with him. It was his way or no way."

"But you went to his funeral."

"Out of respect." She rested a hand over his heart. "Why didn't the judge believe you?"

"Maybe he thought no one could be that dumb. But I could. Was."

"Then why didn't you go to federal prison, too?"

"I wasn't on the surveillance footage. I didn't go in the store. I didn't have a weapon. I didn't resist arrest."

"Rubin ran."

Clay nodded. "Yup. Like a rabbit. But he didn't get far. Gabe is a good runner."

"Played on the track team, right?"

"Mile and quarter mile."

"Rubin was stupid."

"Rubin was scared. We all were. But Rubin was more scared of his father than of prison. He knew his father would beat the hell out of him. His dad didn't even bail him. Just left him there."

"And you had Luke Forrest, FBI agent and decorated US Marine. The papers said he spoke at your hearing."

"He did. Asked for leniency, and he offered the program that accepted me. He was the only one who saw me during those twelve months. No contact, that's one of the rules, but FBI agents don't count, I guess. He got me the job with the tribal livestock manager. Donner is a classmate of his."

Izzie pushed off his arm and straightened. Clay had to fight to not drag her back against him. It had been so long, and he missed her so much.

"Didn't Gabe tell them about how you fought Martin?"

"He didn't see that. It happened fast. Seat blocked most of it. Just my word, which isn't worth much."

"What happened to the girls?"

"Oh, they were out there and they got them, INS and federal agencies. The women were detained, deported."

"You saved them."

"They likely came right back in the next truck."

Izzie rubbed her face with her palm and scooted away from him. "Thank you for telling me," she said.

"Thank you for listening."

They'd gone all formal again. He didn't like it.

Her eyes held a wariness that her smile did not mask. The water was now black and the sky clouding over. A cold wind blew, causing a light chop on the water.

"Best get back. Looks like rain."

Izzie stood and waited for him to rise. They walked back to the truck and slipped into their seats. She turned the key, and the truck rumbled to life. Izzie drove them back to town.

"I was going to sell a few cows to pay the fine, but they tell me I can't get them out while they are in quarantine," said Izzie.

"That's so."

"Do you think they will charge me the detention fee for the days they are in quarantine?"

"Not sure," he said.

"How long do I have to wait for the veterinary report?"

"I've never done this before, so I don't know how long it takes."

"Who takes care of my herd until then?"

"I guess I do," said Clay.

She glanced at him. "You'll see they get what they need?"

"Will do."

He wished she needed more from him than reading sign and watering cattle. He wished he could be the man in whom Izzie confided.

Wished she would hold on to his arm and snuggle up against him again. But there was a mountain of troubles separating them. Talking wouldn't gain back what was lost. She'd left him and he'd left her. But Izzie had asked for his help to get her cows back. He planned to do so, and he knew exactly where to start. Rubin Fox, his old friend and convicted felon, now a full member of the Wolf Posse. If someone was cooking meth up there, Rubin would know about it.

Chapter Ten

It was end of business on Thursday before Clay could find time to go and see Rubin Fox. As he was leaving the office of the livestock manager, Clay noticed Izzie's neighbor in the parking lot. He was about to go over and say hello, but as he moved closer, he saw that Floyd was talking to Franklin Soto, the tribe's livestock inspector.

Soto was in his fifties, short and broad with an athletic physique slowly going soft. He had a ready smile, undeterred by the brown front teeth caused, Clay had heard, by a collision with the thick skull of a cow. Every year, Soto headed up the committee for the annual rodeo, which together with the tribe's casino supplied the operating budget and prize money for the rodeo events. Soto's full-time job was the health and vaccination records of the tribes' cattle, Soto was the go-between with the state officials to be certain the tribe was in compliance with all regulations.

Something about the way that Patch and Soto leaned in and spoke in hushed tones put Clay on alert, and he slowed his approach. Floyd noticed him first and called a greeting. The two men broke apart. Patch headed in Clay's direction while Soto walked past Clay without acknowledging his presence. Happened a lot.

"So, wedding tomorrow?" asked Floyd.

Clay watched Soto pass. What were they up to?

"What?" Clay asked.

"Kino. He's getting married tomorrow."

"Oh, on Saturday. He is."

"She a nice girl?"

Clay watched Soto disappear through the door and considered retracing his steps, but he had to go to a family barbecue tonight, his grandmother's party for Kino before the entire clam headed down to Salt River for the wedding rehearsal and rehearsal dinner on Friday. That meant he had limited time to find Rubin.

"Very nice."

"You got a date?"

Clay shook his head.

"Oh, I thought maybe you and Izzie were back together again, with you helping her and all."

Clay gave another shake of his head. Patch was a terrible fisherman.

"Just as well. That girl is in over her head. Best keep clear of her."

Now Patch had Clay's complete attention. He fixed his gaze on Patch, taking in his slippery smile.

"What does that mean, exactly?"

"Oh, well, just that she's got her mother's debts and those boys to look after. Hard to see how she'll make ends meet, unless she finds a man."

"She's doing okay."

"If you say so. I know exactly how much it costs to raise cattle. And I don't see her selling as many as she'd need to in order to pay her debts. What with her lack of sales and that nonsense up in her pasture, kind of makes me wonder where she found the extra money."

Clay resisted the urge to push Patch on to his scrawny backside. Instead he touched the brim of his hat and forced a smile.

"Gotta go. Family party tonight. Kino's send off."

"Oh, sure. Have fun at the wedding. Reckon half the tribe will be there."

Clay climbed into his truck, letting the anger loose on the innocent vehicle door that closed with such force it shook the interior. Could Izzie possibly be wrapped up in this? Was that why he was so mad? But she wouldn't have asked him to nose around if she were involved…unless she was playing him. Clay felt his shoulders slump. That would just kill him.

Clay turned the key in the ignition. His truck protested and then turned over. Why was he even going to see Rubin? He had no dog in this fight. He should be heading to his place to change for the party. Instead, he turned toward the worst section of the Rez. He hadn't been there since he was a teenager, but the Fox family remained in the trailer that had tilted badly even back then. Well, his mother and two sisters continued to live there and Rubin slept there sometimes. Rubin's father was still in federal prison for trafficking, second conviction, because of the illegal girls that Clay had reported. The case was one of the rare instances where the district attorney had been solicited by the tribal council, and she had agreed to try the case. Rubin's dad was four years into an eight-year sentence, and he and his son had served time in the same prison for a while.

Clay did not expect a warm welcome from the Fox family.

After Rubin had returned to Black Mountain from prison, Clay had seen him around. He'd looked different because he was different. Short hair, gaunt cheeks and a chiseled body that left no hint of the boy who had been sent away. Rubin was dressing like just what he had become—a gang member, with overlarge jeans and shirt that were ideal for concealing a weapon and a flat-brimmed ball cap that shielded his eyes. Clay had told Rubin he was sorry about his dad, and Rubin had sworn at him. Since then they had largely ignored each other. Everyone knew Rubin was a dealer, and he had his own place. But on weeknights, Rubin often ate at home, then went to work with the Wolf Posse. Clay knew that from conversation around his grandmother Glendora's table. Kino wanted to arrest Rubin. Gabe said they didn't have enough evidence.

Clay knocked at the front door. A moment later a beautiful girl stood in the door frame.

"Anna?" he asked, guessing the older of Rubin's sisters.

"Beth," she said and giggled.

Clay shook his head in disbelief. "Is Rubin here?"

"He's at the table. You're Clay Cosen, right?"

"Who?" That was Rubin's mother's voice, full of fury.

His mother started shouting, and Rubin came to the door pushing his sister back and ordering her to the kitchen. She gave Clay a seductive look of regret that made Clay's ears go back.

"Really?" said Rubin. "You come to my house?"

"I need to speak to you." Clay couldn't quite muster the courage to say he needed a favor.

"You got nerve, Cosen. Coming here." Rubin shouted over his shoulder in Apache, telling his mother to hush up. Then he followed Clay out into the night. "Why not come to my crib, coz?"

They both knew why. That's where the Wolf Posse met and conducted business. Clay was less welcome there, if that was possible.

Clay glanced at Rubin, noting that he had added more tattoos to his forearms. Wolves, of course, the symbol of the gang that Clay had come very close to joining before he'd seen that the ones who really had his back had been his family all along. His brothers. His uncle Luke. Where would he be now without them? He looked at Rubin, and a chill slithered up his spine. Rubin, a dark mirror, reflecting what might have been.

"You and I got no biz-nus, bro. How 'bout you blow?" Rubin placed a hand on the door handle, barring the entrance to his mother's home.

"I need to ask a question."

Rubin lifted a brow, curious now.

"Do you know what's going on up in Izzie's pasture?"

Rubin snorted and then gave a cruel smile. "'Course I know."

"Can you tell me?"

"What? You might be wearing a wire. You think I'm loco?"

"I'm trying to help her."

"Oh yeah? Like you helped me after the robbery? You had a lawyer, a fed and a cop in your corner. You helped me all right. Pinned the whole thing right here." He poked his chest with his thumb.

Clay was about to remind his friend that he had been innocent of every crime except being a damned fool and believing his friends. Instead Clay remained silent.

Rubin pursed his lips and then rolled his eyes. When his gaze came back to meet Clay's the bravado was gone, and his expression was deadly serious.

"You asking me and I can't tell you. But I can tell you this, stay away from Isabella Nosie. You hang around her, and you'll get yourself into trouble worse than the last time."

"What does that mean? Is Izzie involved?"

"Get off my porch, bro. And stay away from Izzie." Rubin stepped back into the house and slammed the door in his face.

Clay stood in the cool night air, feeling a different kind of cold seep into his blood. *Stay away from her.* Was Izzie involved or in trouble? Clay returned to his truck, wishing he could follow Rubin's advice and knowing that he could not.

He didn't really remember the drive to his grandmother's because his mind was elsewhere. All Rubin had done was warn him off. But it was more than Rubin had done the last time.

Clay completely forgot that he was expected

for the party at his grandmother's until he drove past her house and saw the gathering of people in the yard. Tomorrow afternoon the family would head down to Salt River Reservation to meet the bride's family. Tonight, their grandmother wanted all her boys together for one last meal. Clay hung a U-turn and pulled into the overcrowded drive. Clyne's large SUV sat before him, Gabe's unmarked unit and Kino's patrol cruiser. Off on the lawn was his grandmother's late-model blue Ford sedan with the crumpled back fender where she'd backed into a concrete pole.

There were two fires in the side yard, one for cooking and one for gathering. In the firelight, Clay could make out several of Kino's friends and a few of Clyne's and Gabe's. None of his, of course, because he had forgotten to invite any of the guys from work.

From the looks of things, the party was already started. He glanced at the clock on his dashboard and winced. He was an hour late.

Glendora spotted him first and left the cooking pit. She met Clay as he exited his truck.

"Where have you been?" she asked.

"I had to see a friend."

She looked at his empty cab. "But you didn't bring him. You have the drinks?"

Clay's heart sank. He'd forgotten his one job, to pick up the pop from the beverage center. His grandmother read the truth on his face. Man, would he ever stop being the family screw-up?

"Clay?" she asked.

"I'm sorry. I'll go get it."

She clasped his wrist in a hold stronger than he would have expected from a woman her age. But then she had raised four boys after his parents had died. Clay didn't know anyone as mentally strong as Glendora, and that was including his four brothers.

"No. They'll drink water and beer. You're not leaving now."

They walked toward the makeshift banquet table, which was a large piece of plywood on sawhorses that had been covered with a blue flowered bedsheet. There was so much food he feared the table might collapse, but on further inspection, he saw that his brothers had braced the plywood with two-by-fours because they had been here early to set up.

Clay heaved a sigh as his grandmother tugged him toward the gathering.

It was fitting that they come together here, of course, in the yard where every important event of their lives had been celebrated.

His grandmother clung to Clay's arm as they moved toward the yard. There were Clyne and Gabe, tending the ribs, basting and turning. The ribs would likely be dry as they had been cooking much longer than expected. Beside them, in a circle of friends, stood Kino, laughing.

"Doesn't Kino look happy?" said his grandmother.

"Very."

"Who would have guessed that my youngest boy would marry first?" She slapped Clay. "What's wrong with the rest of you? Clyne is thirty-two and so busy with tribal business he hasn't dated in a year, and Gabe, always running from one emergency to the next. When does he have time to see a woman? You all have good jobs. Why don't you find a girl?" She sighed and looped her arm through his, leaning on his shoulder. "Kino and Lea are a good match. Do you know her Apache name?"

His grandmother referred to the name given to Lea by the shaman on the last day of her Sunrise Ceremony. Kino had told him Lea's formal name, but he could not recall. But he knew Izzie's. She was called Medicine Root Woman. It was a powerful name, grounded to the earth with a touch of magic in the strong medicine. Izzie was strong, he knew, for only someone so tough could carry the responsibility she bore.

"It is Bright Star Woman, and Lea is bright and giving. She is the balance Kino needs to keep him from seeing the world as full of nothing but bad people. Forgiveness and justice, a good match."

Was his grandmother referring to his brother's relentless hunt for their father's murderer? Clay had gone along to protect Kino, but not for any need for vengeance. His father had given them life, but he was a bad person in many ways. Much of Clay's anger had come from knowing exactly what his father was and did.

"You need balance, too."

"I'm balanced."

His grandmother patted his hand in a pacifying way. "Maybe you can take a few days off and go up to South Dakota with them."

"Grandmother, I'm not joining Kino on his honeymoon."

"But if you go, then they can have a real honeymoon instead of following your sister's trail, visiting with Bureau of Indian Affairs and the foster family we know had her as a baby. You should go instead of Kino and Lea."

"I'm not a police officer."

"You are his brother. You're smart and the best tracker on the reservation. You might even be as good as your grandfather Hex Clawson and better than my father."

That made Clay's eyebrows lift in surprise. This was high praise indeed.

"Jovanna has left no tracks."

"Everything that moves leaves tracks," she said, repeating the words Clay had heard many times and used often himself. "My husband taught me that."

"Yes, Grandmother. But I have work here."

Glendora slipped her hand from the crook of his arm. "What work is more important than finding your sister?"

Keeping Izzie safe, Clay thought.

His grandmother waited, but when Clay did not reply she exhaled and then motioned toward the gathering. "Come on, before those ribs are as leathery as jerked beef."

They moved just outside the fire's light.

"Look who's here," called his grandmother.

He was received with hugs and hoots and slaps on the back. Finally someone handed him a beer. Nice to be treated like the guest of honor instead of the lost sheep.

Kino stepped forward and hugged him.

His younger brother released him and asked, "Everything all right?"

"Sure, sure. Congratulations."

Kino gave a half smile and still managed to look happier than Clay had ever seen him.

"Good thing you didn't shoot her that day you met," said Clay.

Kino gave him a playful slug to the arm.

"Hey, quiet about that."

They exchanged a smile. Kino was getting

married. The thought struck him, and Clay's heart gave a funny little flutter.

Kino's friends circled closer, returning to their conversations interrupted by his arrival. There was Bill and Javier, his brother's two closest friends. Kino's bride-to-be, Lea Altaha, was with her family at Salt River, making this a low-key bachelor's party. The woman Kino would marry was also the one he had rescued from the cartels down on the border three months earlier. Lea had worked with an aid organization, providing drinking water to those illegals crossing the desert. As Shadow Wolves, he and Kino had been charged with tracking and apprehending those same illegals. Yet somehow the two had set aside their differences and made a good, strong match.

Clay went to joint Clyne and Gabe. Clyne offered a smile, but Gabe, less tolerant of Clay's general lack of regard for the time, cast him a look of disappointment.

"Here he is. At last," said Clyne. "I'm famished." He was the one who played well with others and who was a master at both negotiation and consensus building. A leader by any measure.

Gabe, ever the investigator, was more to the point. "Where have you been?"

"I had to stop by to see a friend."

Gabe's brow swept down over his dark eyes. "What friend?"

Clay changed the subject. "Any word on the dead cattle?"

Gabe looked to the heavens as if for patience, then flicked his gaze back to Clay. "You were with Izzie Nosie?"

"No. But—"

"Good. Because you can't work for her and keep your job. You know that, right? Conflict of interest."

"She asked me to do her a favor."

"And you've done it. So stay away from her."

Clay felt the need to challenge, but a glance toward the banquet table showed his grandmother watching them from a distance with worried eyes.

"Anything from the necropsy?" he asked, hoping the dead cattle might prove his suspicions.

Gabe's face went expressionless. "Clay, you do not want to get in the middle of my investigation. And that is what this is, an active investigation. Keep out of it."

He didn't remind Gabe that it was only an investigation because Clay had tracked the cattle, found the dead cows and called him.

"You hear me?" asked Gabe.

"I do." Clay could turn his back on just about anyone and anything. But not family and not Izzie. He felt like a deer being tugged in opposite directions by two hungry wolves. Someone was about to be disappointed. But either way, the deer lost.

Chapter Eleven

Izzie had a call in at nine on Monday morning to the state veterinary offices. As an interested party, listed on their report, she was entitled to a copy of their findings, and even though Clay had raised the possibility, she was still speechless when she heard the results.

All three necropsy reports indicated that her cows died of complete cardiopulmonary collapse. There was fluid in their lungs and irritation of all respiratory membranes. The cattle also showed extreme kidney and liver damage. Blood work revealed low blood potassium and high levels of magnesium.

"Consistent with poisoning," finished the vet on the phone. "Want a fax copy or US mail?"

"What caused this?" asked Izzie.

A pause, then, "Ah, we are turning this over to the FBI. You might want to contact an attorney."

Izzie gripped the phone, blinking like an owl as that bit of information settled in. She'd never been in trouble a day in her life. She'd always done exactly what was expected even when she wanted to do otherwise.

"But I didn't do anything," she said.

"Is there anything else?"

"No. I... Thank you."

"Yeah. I'll drop a copy in the mail. We have your address." The vet hung up, leaving Izzie gripping a phone connected to no one.

Dizziness rocked her, and she had to sit down hard in one of the vinyl-cushioned chairs at her mother's kitchen table. Next she set the phone on the plastic tablecloth festooned with yellow daisies and used the same hand to wipe the sweat away from her forehead.

Clay had been right. Those cows had inhaled something that had come out of those trailers, something that had stopped their hearts.

Izzie folded her arms on the table and rested her head on her arms. She closed her eyes. Poison, drugs, Clay had said. Something popped into her mind, and she lifted up from the table so fast she swayed.

"Clay was right! They *were* poisoned. And I have proof."

They had to give her the cattle back.

Izzie drew on her denim jacket and headed for her truck. Thirty-three minutes later she was standing in front of Dale Donner's desk demanding that he release her cows.

Donner eyed her from behind a battered, overladen desk, tipping back in his swivel chair. She recalled that her father had been happy at Donner's appointment, saying he was a fair man. His shirt stretched a little too tight over his belly, and his hands gripped the arms as if deciding if he should take the trouble to get up or not. "My cows?" she said again. "State vet says they are not contagious."

"Well, I don't have that report yet," said Donner, sounding peeved.

"Call and get it faxed. I'll wait."

He lifted his brows. "That could take a while."

She wondered if she might have had better results if she had tried a different approach. More honey and less vinegar. But she had already set herself down this road, and it was too late to backtrack.

"I want my cows back."

"I'm sure you do. But you can't have them until I have the report, and then you still owe a fine on the ones we rounded up off the road."

"But someone cut my fences and chased those cattle out of my pastures."

"I don't have the police report corroborating that, and even if I did, you have to file an appeal." Donner pushed his desk chair back and rolled on castors to the filing cabinet, where he retrieved the appropriate form. He used his legs like a child on a scooter to return to her and handed over the pages. "My advice is that you pay the fine, get your cattle back and then file the appeal. If it goes through, we'll reimburse you."

She didn't want to do that because it involved selling her cattle, which took time and cost her money. "How long do appeals take?"

"Well, you have a right to a hearing in tribal court, but you have to make a petition for a hearing within three business days of notice of impoundment, and that would be today. You just made it."

She opened her mouth to protest, but he just kept talking.

"Once the tribal court officer gets that form—" he pointed to the pages now gripped in her hand "—then the tribal court has seven business days to hear your request. Let's see, that's by next Tuesday at the latest, but they don't meet on Tuesday. So Wednesday it is. Now you have to have evidence. Can't just be your word. Witnesses and physical evidence is best. Police report, surely. Vet report and anything else you can think of."

"But you can't sell my cattle in the meantime?"

"Twenty days after notice of impoundment. We hold auctions every Thursday. Let's see." Donner consulted the business half of the wall calendar on the overcrowded bulletin board behind him. "That's October eighth."

Izzie wanted to ask where Clay might be, but resisted. She filled out the paperwork while she waited. When the fax machine chirped to life, Donner collected the pages and made a copy for himself.

"I can release the quarantined lot. Not the impounded ones, though."

"You'll bring them to my place."

Donner rubbed his neck. "You have to arrange transport."

Izzie's face went hot. "But you took them."

"As a precaution."

She flapped her arms, and the appeal fluttered against her leg. "Fine. I'll be back."

She stomped from the office and took both the appeal application and fax pages across the street to tribal headquarters.

After that, Izzie took Donner's advice and spoke to Victor Bustros about selling a few of her cattle at Thursday's auction to pay the impoundment fine and hoped she get it back on appeal. Victor Bustros handled the brand inspection and auctions on the Rez. Izzie calculated carefully how many of the cattle she needed to sell to and pointed out the cattle picked to Bustros's assistant, who marked them with paint. She hoped they got a fair price, because her checking account was dangerously low. She wondered, not for the first time, what her mother spent the grocery money on, because for a cattle family, they certainly ate a lot of beans.

Since Izzie did not have the extra money to have her recovered cattle trucked back home, she was left with only one alternative. She called her part-time hands, Max Reyes and Eli Beach. They arrived with the horse trailer and three of her horses, including Biscuit.

The rest of the day was spent moving the released portion of her herd slowly from the quarantine yard to her permitted grazing land.

By day's end she was hot, hungry and angry at no one and everyone. She thanked Eli and Max, who agreed to go retrieve the horse trailer while she saw the horses settled. It wasn't until she returned to the house, bone tired and dragging her feet with fatigue, that her mother stepped from the front door and greeted her with a worried expression. She extended her arm, offering a white legal-sized envelope.

"This came for you. I had to sign for it."

Izzie studied the tribal stamp and seal. Her mother had not opened it.

"What is it?" she asked.

"Might be the necropsy results or the official release from quarantine. Could be their acknowledgment. I've requested a hearing about the cut fences. I don't think I should have to pay a fine when someone is messing with me." Izzie slit the envelope with her finger, leaving a ragged flap of torn paper. Then she drew out the enclosed letter. She scanned the page. Her ears started ringing.

"No, no, no," she whispered. She reread the words to be sure she understood, and then her arm dropped to her side, still clutching the letter.

"What is it?"

"Notice from the general livestock coordinator."

"Pizarro?"

Izzie nodded. "They have scheduled our pastures for immediate renourishment."

"What does that mean?"

Izzie stared at her mother. "It means the cows can't graze here."

Her mother shrugged. "Good. Sell the damned things. I hate cows."

With that her mother left her only daughter standing alone in the yard. Izzie managed to wait until her mother was out of sight before she began bawling like a newly branded cow.

How was she going to keep the cattle for her brothers if she had no place to graze the herd?

Izzie retreated to the barn and her favorite horse, Biscuit. She held Biscuit's coarse mane and wept for a good long while as Biscuit listened to Izzie pour out her problems. Her horse knew more about Izzie than any person living, though all secrets were safe with her mare. It was only after she had cried herself out that she realized that something stunk, figuratively.

First her cattle were rustled to the road, then three cows were poisoned by something that stopped their hearts, and then, on the very day she got half of her cattle back, she lost her grazing rights.

"Who pulled those permits, Biscuit?" Izzie asked.

Chapter Twelve

The Monday after Kino's wedding, Clay found himself back in the saddle assigned to the tribe's communal herd and the task of separating mothers and yearlings for calf branding. The job was taxing but he thought his weariness stemmed more from the festivities than from the work. The wedding was beautiful and he'd enjoyed himself. But today, unexpectedly, the memories of the celebration filled him with an unforeseen melancholy. He wished Izzie had been there with him. If he had asked, would she have come?

The day was cold with a gusty wind that lifted stinging bits of sand and dirt. Clay drew up his red kerchief over his mouth and nose and refocused on the mother who had cut away, bringing her back with the others. She and her twins trotted through the shoot into the correct pen. Roger Tolino worked the shoot, closing them in and Clay swung round for another target, but his mind still lingered on the wedding.

Clyne had no date, either. His eldest brother had said that it was one thing to take a woman out on Saturday night but quite another to invite her to your brother's wedding. Clyne did not want to give any of the women he dated the idea that he was interested in more than a night's diversion. Clyne was a strange guy, very vested in tradition and community, yet unable to find an Apache woman who stirred him in more than the obvious places. He'd even been up to Oklahoma a time or two on business that Clay suspected involved opportunities for more than just tribal networking.

Clay wondered what Izzie would say about that. He imagined all the things that he wanted to tell her about Lea and Kino. How they met as adversaries and now were newlyweds. It gave him hope.

Clay worked his way through the morning surrounded by the bawling of calves and shouts of the men. The pounding of their hooves reminded Clay of the women's pounding feet as they danced in a circle at his little brother's reception.

The wedding had been a wonderful celebration, with a mix of a church service and Apache dancing and song. Clay had been so proud to stand with his brothers at the altar and witness the match, but was surprised by all the unexpected emotions that his little brother's wedding stirred.

His brother Gabe was the only one of them to

bring a date. He had gone with his usual go-to for such occasions, Melissa Turno, a classmate and assistant to the director of the Tribal Museum. His older brother had not had a serious relationship since his fiancée, Selena Dosela, had broken their engagement immediately after Gabe had arrested her father.

Unlike Gabe, who played it safe, or Clyne, who didn't play at all, Clay *wanted* to give Izzie the wrong idea. But he didn't think she felt the same.

Still, he couldn't stop thinking about how much he would have liked to see her dance with the women of the Salt River Reservation while he beat the drum and sang with his brothers. How he would have been proud to bring her as his date. To show everyone that she was his girl. Only she wasn't. Might never be.

Clay sighted the low gray clouds sweeping in, predicting a change in the weather. He was glad he had his fleece coat and lined gloves.

After lunch they started the task of checking the mother's brands and collecting the right irons. Each member of the tribe with cattle had a registered brand and those families with only a cow or two often preferred to keep them in the communal herd.

Donner's men worked well as a team. Matching the brands, roping, tying. Since Roger Tolino was the slightest and least competent with a rope, he had the job of sorting and branding. That left Clay and Dodge to catch and rope the calves and Tolino to let them go. Clay liked roping and riding, and usually such days passed quickly. But today even the coffee could not erase his general buzz of fatigue.

Clay took off after another calf, but, maybe because of the wedding, he couldn't stop fantasizing about what it would be like to go away with Izzie and then return to make a home. Not that Izzie wanted to play house with him, and the truth was, if he didn't quit messing with her, he might lose his job.

He roped the next calf, and his horse backed up, making the rope tight and his job of flipping the yearling to his side much easier. He placed a knee on the furry side and expertly tied the front and one back leg together. Then he stood and dusted off his jeans before retrieving his lariat.

He glanced at the sun and realized they'd be quitting soon. Donner did not pay overtime. Clay turned to the north and wondered how far the newlyweds had gotten. They planned to stop in Denver for two nights and then visit Yellowstone on their way east to South Dakota.

His grandmother had tried once more to get Clay to head up there first and track their sister. He closed his eyes and imagined what that little girl of three would look like now as a child of twelve. Would she have their mother's high arching brow or the broad nose of their father? Did she wear her hair to her waist or in a short, modern style? An image of a teen with a blue stripe of dyed hair caused him to growl, as he mounted his horse.

His boss showed up to watch. Clay heard him calling something like, "So you decided to work for me today, did you?" Clay just waved and kept riding. Keeping his head down and his seat in the saddle.

When he finished work, he might go tell Izzie that even her neighbor, Patch, was gossiping about her mom's debts. He hoped her troubles had not caused her to do something stupid. If there was anyone who knew more about doing something stupid than him, Clay had yet to meet them. He knew Izzie was smarter than he was, but desperation could cause even a good girl to go bad. Honestly, he would have used any excuse to see her again. Pathetic, he thought.

Donner called a halt, and Clay turned his horse toward the communal pasture. His mount would get some extra grain, and he'd curry him down before turning him loose with the others.

Then he'd head back to his empty house to shower and change. This morning, with Kino gone, the place had been unnaturally quiet. And he'd had the misfortune of having to drink his own coffee. He wondered if Izzie made good coffee. Then he wondered how he might get Izzie over to his empty house and keep her there until morning. He needed to separate his fantasy world from his real life, where Izzie needed only his help. That didn't mean she needed *him*. Not the way he needed her, anyway.

Clay tied up his horse and removed the saddle, carrying it to his truck and then returning to curry the horse's sweaty barrel, his strokes rhythmic and practiced.

Izzie had been in trouble, and she had called him. Him. That meant something, right? She had not let her mother's dictates control her. And he had helped her, hadn't he? Maybe there could be more between them. Maybe she was the one person outside his family who was willing to give him a second chance.

He'd left the marriage ceremony hopeful. But now the doubts had caught up with him. First, Izzie was too good for him. Second, she might be playing him.

He said goodbye to the others, turning down an offer to join them for supper. He walked stiffly back to his truck, grit covered, dirty and satisfied that he had earned his pay.

Diego Azar pulled in beside his truck. Diego was a few years younger with a persistent five o'clock shadow and a bushy mustache. His father was Mexican, giving him more beard and less height than the rest of them. Nice guy and one of the first to befriend Clay. Today he'd been manning the office so Donner could get out in the field.

The younger man's excited expression said he had news. Clay paused, waiting.

"We got the report on the cattle."

He perked up. Clay knew what cattle, but he asked just to be sure. "Izzie's cattle?"

"Yeah. They were released this morning from quarantine."

"Why didn't they call me? I could have driven them back."

Azar nibbled the ends of one side of his mustache as if considering his reply. "Donner said you'd ask that. So he told me to tell you that if he catches you moonlighting for her again, he'll fire you."

Clay stilled. He needed this job, but more than that he needed the clean reputation that came with working for a man like Mr. Donner. In addition, it would be poor thanks to his uncle if he lost this position.

"She hasn't asked me to do anything else." Which was the truth, much to his chagrin. "When does she get her herd?"

"Already did. Some, anyway. They're keeping the strays we impounded from the road. Let loose the rest. She drove them out this morning."

"Drove? You mean we didn't offer to return them?"

"Guess not. Owner's responsibility. Right?"

Clay took a step toward Azar, who raised his hands in surrender. "Hey, not my call, man. Donner was there."

Clay knew they often used the tribe's vehicles to transport private stock. But not Izzie's cattle.

Clay looked toward Donner, who was talking to Tolino and Dodge. Clay resisted the urge to march over there. Donner met his eye, held it and then returned to his conversation.

"Oh," said Azar. "Almost forgot. He told me to give you this." Azar withdrew several neatly folded pages from his breast pocket. "He said I should wait while you read it."

Clay accepted the offering, unfolding the pages. It was the necropsy report from the state. Another glance showed Donner watching him like a raven from the top of a tall pine. Clay turned his attention to the report.

"It's bad stuff, Cosen. Really, really bad."

Clay scanned the results. The long and short of it was that the cattle had been poisoned, and the poison had been phosphine, a by-product of cooking crystal meth. He glanced from the report to meet Donner's expressionless stare.

Donner ambled over.

Clay folded the pages and offered them back to Donner as Azar looked from one man to another.

"Thank you," said Clay.

"Figured you'd get a hold of it one way or another."

Did he mean from Izzie or Gabe, or was he insinuating that Clay would resort to theft? He didn't know, and let the comment slide. But he didn't like the implication.

Donner accepted the report and thrust it in his back pocket. "I've already called Chief Cosen to notify him of the cause of death. He's bringing in the FBI. You need to stay way the heck away from this."

"This or her?"

Donner rubbed his neck. "You work for me, so I have to say it because you don't have a reputation for being the best judge of character."

And there it was. "No one tells me who I can and can't speak to. Not even my boss." But his skin was now tingling, and the hairs on his neck stood up just the same way they had that day when he'd looked in his rearview mirror and seen his brother's police cruiser with lights flashing.

He turned to go and Donner spoke again.

"Clay, they think she's involved."

There was a whooshing sound in his ears now. Had Izzie become so desperate that she would allow such things to happen on her land? He didn't want to believe it. But his stomach cramped with his doubts. He never would have thought Martin would have picked up a gun and shot an innocent man just so he could get laid. How could Clay really know what was in the heart of a man?

Or a woman?

Donner headed in the opposite direction, leaving Azar hovering with wide worried eyes.

"I gotta go," said Clay.

Clay climbed into his truck and pulled the door closed. Azar stepped forward and gripped the ledge of the open window.

"Why don't you come have a drink with us?" asked Azar.

"Rain check, okay?"

Azar released his hold and stepped back. "Be careful, Clay."

Chapter Thirteen

Supper time approached, and Izzie was still in the barn with Biscuit. She'd curried her horse down, cleaned the tack and wiped her eyes before her brothers piled off the bus. They'd headed to the house to change and grab a snack, but then they'd return dressed in work clothes and buzzing with excitement over the return of half the herd. That gave her a chance to pull her work shirt over the documents in her back pocket that revoked the family's permits and to practice her expression-less mask of stoicism. It was easier than forcing a smile and easier on the boys than crying in front of them.

"You got them back," shouted Will, by way of a greeting as he charged into the barn.

At eleven, he was one of the tallest in the sixth grade, but also one of the thinnest. All arms and legs, he did not yet resemble their father for whom he was named. He wore his hair very short, as was the style now for boys. Behind him came

Jerry, a fourth grader, who was losing teeth but not yet gaining inches. As a result he was more coordinated and compact.

Izzie kept brushing, hoping that her brothers would be so preoccupied with the cattle, now filling the pasture behind their home, that they would not notice their sister's red and puffy eyes.

"Yes, most of them," she said, thinking her voice sounded nearly normal.

Will stood in the barn door, looking up at the hillside and the herd that grazed as if they had not ever left. Jerry reached her side, his eyes dancing with excitement.

"How did you do it?"

"The report came back from the state. They're not sick."

"So what killed the three we lost?"

Izzie had thought about this, wondering how much to tell them. She wanted to protect them but did not want to leave them ill-equipped to deal with what their classmates might hear from their parents. They were still children. How much did they really need to know?

"Well, nothing catching. That's the important thing." She glanced down from Biscuit's withers and met Jerry's gaze. "How about you two see to the sheep. I'll feed the horses today."

"Hurray!" shouted Jerry, pumping his fist as if

he'd just scored the game-winning basket. Then he wheeled away.

"Don't forget the chickens!" she shouted to their backs.

Izzie prepared four buckets of oats and some vitamins. She placed Biscuit's feed before her and headed out to the pasture. At sight of the buckets the other three horses came trotting back to the barn for supper. That was where she was when she saw a familiar rusty pickup pull into her drive.

Clay, she realized, and her heart did a little flutter. He swung out of the cab and strode in her direction. She breathed deep for the first time since the papers were delivered. The dread, which she carried since receiving that envelope, began to slip away.

"Heard about your cattle," he said by way of a greeting.

"Yeah." She tried for a smile but fell short, managing only a grimace.

"And the report. The cows weren't sick." He reached her now, and only the thin wire fence separated them.

Izzie glanced toward the house, wondering if her mother stood at the window, watching. Izzie's stomach knotted tighter, and her need to touch him warred with the worry that her mother would embarrass her. She shouldn't care, but her mother thought him responsible for Martin's death. Martin, Izzie's mother believed, was a good boy who had paid with his life for his involvement with Clay. If she only knew the truth. But there was no point in arguing. She would not believe a word Izzie said.

"Would you rather they be sick?" he asked. He was studying her face, and his expression was as somber as a funeral mourner. He lifted a hand and placed one gloved finger under her chin, tilting her face upward. "Izzie, have you been crying?"

He noticed. Of course he did. Clay had always noticed everything about her. A new shirt, a change in mood. Her eyes started to burn again.

She drew back a step and nodded. Then she pulled the papers from her back pocket and offered them to Clay. "I got these today."

He took them and read them as the horses finished their meal and ambled back into the pasture. Izzie retrieved the buckets and placed them by the fence, then slipped out between the wires, expertly missing the barbs both top and bottom. She noticed Will and Jerry leaving the chicken coop and pausing to stare at their unexpected visitor. Will started toward them.

Clay lowered the pages. "Immediate renourishment?"

The knot filled her throat again, so she nodded.

"What's this about? You've had this grazing permit forever."

Actually since her grandfather had applied for them, back when no one wanted this far-off corner of the Rez. Her grandfather and father had cleared many of the trees by hand, making the wooded area suitable for grazing.

"Maybe it's just time," she offered.

"No way, Izzie. This has to do with the state report. You know that, don't you?"

Before she could answer, Will and Jerry drew up, hands in back pockets, trying to look like the men of the place.

"Ya'atch," said Clay, using the Apache greeting.

They both answered in unison.

"Boys, this is Clay Cosen."

Jerry's eyes went wide, and he and Will exchanged looks. Clearly it was a name they knew.

"Clay and I went to school together."

The two stood staring like two baby owls.

"Well? Shake his hand," she ordered.

Jerry, the outgoing one, offered his hand first. Her brother stared at his hand while Clay shook, as if expecting something to happen. Then Will offered his, and Clay accepted it.

"You two done with your chores?" she asked.

"Not yet," said Will.

"Best get to them. Daylight's burning."

They hesitated and then walked toward the sheep pen, casting several backward glances.

"Afraid to leave you alone with me, I'll bet," said Clay.

"They're only boys," she said, dismissing his concerns.

"They're your brothers. No matter how old they are, they want to protect you."

"I think this is a bigger threat," she said, retrieving the papers.

"I'd say so. What do you plan to do?"

"I'm not sure. Apply for a new permit?"

Clay shook his head. "You can fight it, you know?"

She didn't know that and told him so with her blank stare.

"You appeal to the council. Call the office and ask to be placed on the agenda. They're meeting Wednesday night."

"I can't speak before the council."

"Why not?"

"I just… I've never done anything like that before."

"Izzie, you're under attack here. Half your herd is still impounded. Three were poisoned, and now your permits have been pulled. Am I the only one who smells a rat?"

He'd confirmed her fears. The tears started again, running down her cheeks as her lip trembled like a seismometer predicting an earthquake.

Clay pulled her in his arms. His hand rubbed her back, and he made soothing sounds. That only made her cry harder because it felt so good to be back in his embrace again.

"I got you, Izzie. I'll get you through this."

She sagged against him, letting him take her weight and her fear and her sorrow. He took it all, standing solid as Black Mountain as he cradled her. She finally reined herself in and straightened to find both her brothers staring at them from across the yard. She stepped back from Clay, and he cast a glance over his shoulder. Then he returned his attention to her.

"You're going to be all right?"

She didn't think so. Everything around her seemed to be breaking loose, and she couldn't hold the pieces together any longer. She should go and reassure the boys. Tell them that everything was all right. But it wasn't all right. It was so *not* all right.

"I'll talk to Clyne and make sure you get on the agenda," said Clay and inclined his head toward the house. "You want me to stay?"

She did. So much it frightened her.

"No. Call me, please."

"Have you seen the state report yet—the necropsy?"

"No. I heard a summary over the phone."

"Call my boss. Ask for a copy. You're entitled to one. And I'll see if I can get it."

She didn't even remember walking him to his truck. He took hold of her hand. The act was as natural as breathing. She laced her fingers with his, cherishing the warmth of his palm pressed to hers. Suddenly she didn't feel all alone. It was just like before this all happened. Back when the world was full of nothing but anticipation for their bright future. She looked up at him, taller now, changed in ways she couldn't even imagine. His smile was endearing and made her heart beat faster. How had she ever managed all this time without him? Izzie didn't know. But she did know that she didn't want to do that again.

He released her hand and climbed behind the wheel.

"I'll call tonight."

"Thank you." She waved him away and then walked past her brothers, who gawked at her. She made it into the house to find her mother, redfaced with fury.

It was a confrontation that was long overdue. But this time, Izzie would not turn tail like a whipped dog.

Chapter Fourteen

Clay arrived late for dinner at his grandmother's home. He stepped into the living room and was greeted with the aroma of onions and garlic and beef. The heavenly blend reminded him how long it had been since he'd eaten. His grandmother appeared from the kitchen doorway, face bright with her smile. In her hands she held a wet dish towel showing she had already cleaned up. Clay hugged her, and she patted his shoulder, still clutching the rag.

"You're late," she said. She stood on her tiptoes and inhaled. "You smell good." Now she stepped back, still holding him by each upper arm and beaming up at him. "Showered, dressed. I hope that isn't all for me."

He recalled a time when her face had creased with disappointment in him. He never wanted to see that expression again. Glendora Clawson had already seen more than her share of tragedy, and it showed on her lined face and the silver strands in her dark hair.

"I stopped by to see Izzie."

Gabe appeared from the dining room, pausing in the doorway, an empty coffee mug held absently in one hand and a tight expression on his face.

Clay returned his attention to his grandmother.

"Have you eaten?" she asked.

Clay shook his head, and Glendora went to work, darting into the kitchen. Clay followed, watching her bustle to the cupboards and then to the stove, ladling out a portion of stew from a steaming pot.

"Just let me warm up the fry bread." She set aside the stew and recovered three large disks of the fried dough that all her boys loved. The golden flat bread was wrapped in paper towels and popped in the microwave. She handed over the stew in a bowl with a large spoon.

"Coffee, water or milk?"

"Water, please," said Clay.

She motioned him toward the dining room. Gabe followed a moment later with a steaming cup of coffee. That and the uniform he still wore meant his brother was working tonight.

Clay took the seat adjoining Gabe's. Behind Clay sat a small television on a wobbly table. A weather girl from Phoenix reported clear skies and cold nights.

"Can I get a copy of the state vet report on Izzie's cows?" asked Clay.

Gabe glanced from the television back to him. "Public record."

"Do you have it?"

Gabe fiddled with his phone and then glanced up. "Emailed as an attachment."

"Thanks."

No moss ever grew on Gabe.

From the kitchen came the long plaintiff beep of the microwave and the sound of the door opening. His grandmother appeared with three thick pieces of fry bread. She gave Clay two and Gabe one.

"I had supper," said Gabe.

"Not enough. You're too skinny. All of you." Glendora returned the salt and pepper to the table before Clay and pushed the butter closer. Then she retreated to the kitchen, leaving Gabe and Clay alone.

"Is Luke coming?" asked Clay and then dug into the stew.

"Yeah." Gabe sipped his coffee. "Oh, and he's bringing his new partner, Cassidy something. They were reassigned as a team and have agreed to review my investigation."

Most tribal police were loath to bring in the

federal authorities. Not Gabe. He knew when they were needed, and he didn't hesitate.

"Is Izzie under investigation?"

Gabe gave him a blank stare and lifted his mug, taking a long swallow.

No answer is still an answer, their mother used to say.

"Luke wants to speak to you, too."

Clay nodded, shoveling the stew now, barely tasting the warm, delicious mixture as his famine took control. When he straightened, his grandmother appeared and retrieved the bowl. Clay tore into the fry bread.

"Might be best to keep away from Izzie until they clear her."

Clay sighed, knowing that once again, he wouldn't do what was best or wise or expected. His grandmother returned with another full bowl of stew, and Clay dug in, savoring this helping now that the hunger had eased. Finally he pushed the bowl away and regarded his brother.

"She's not cooking meth," said Clay.

"What if she just gets paid to look the other way?" His brother was a good investigator, and his suspicion worried Clay deeply. He was paid to get to the bottom of things. Sometimes that made him a real pain in the neck. Clay knew for a fact that it was Gabe's unwillingness to ignore things that had broken up his engagement to Selena Dosela. He just had to poke around, and Selena must have felt that he had used her, which he had and would always do to solve a crime. Clay knew Gabe would do his job even if that meant arresting his brother, again.

"If she's involved, then why ask me to track those cows?"

"A mistake, maybe," said Gabe. "Or unrelated."

"Why go up in the woods where they were cooking, and why would they shoot at her?"

"Didn't recognize her?"

"Or she's innocent."

Gabe dropped his police chief persona and gave Clay a worried look. "Don't put me through this again."

"I haven't done anything."

"I still believe you didn't do anything the last time. But being in the wrong place at the wrong time was enough. Remember?"

Clay nodded and went into the kitchen. Clyne appeared from the hall leading to his bedroom and stopped when he noticed Clay.

"Moving back?"

"Not today."

Clyne nodded and rummaged in the refrigerator for a bottle of beer. Clearly Clyne was off duty for the night. Unlike Gabe, Clyne's schedule was regular, except for the occasional emergency, but often they called the tribal council chair first.

His grandmother stowed away the leftovers as Clyne leaned against the counter regarding Clay. *Oh, boy*, Clay thought. *Here comes the other barrel of the Clyne-Gabe shotgun. Two-on-one, that's how it was and always has been.*

"I need you to put Izzie on the council agenda. She is contesting the impoundment and fine."

"Okay."

"She is also contesting her permits being pulled."

Clyne set aside his beer, and Glendora stopped shuffling. Gabe propped himself in the doorway, all ears. Clay told him about the renourishment, and Gabe chimed in about getting the orders from Tessay and delivering them in person, as required.

"I forgot about that," said Clyne absently. "Voted last week on all renourishment recommendations."

"Last week?" asked Gabe, eyes sharp.

Clay caught Clyne and Gabe exchanging a look.

"I'll make a motion for a delay," said Clyne, "if you promise to keep away from that upper pasture."

"Deal," said Clay. The trail would be cold, anyway. "You know that road on her upper pasture? The one in the woods?"

"Yeah."

"Can you find out who built it and why?"

"I'll give it a shot."

"Thanks."

Clyne retrieved his beer, and Clay headed to the living room to call Izzie. She sounded stressed but refused his offer to meet somewhere. He got her email address and agreed to send over the necropsy report. As he returned the receiver to the cradle he worried over the tension that had rung clear in her voice.

Clay wished he could see her, but he abided by her wishes and headed home alone. The house was dark and unnaturally quiet. He wasn't used to being alone, except in the woods, of course, where he preferred it.

On Tuesday they finished the branding. That night Clay ate with his brothers at his grandmother's home. Kino called during their dinner hour to check in. They expected to be in South Dakota by Friday. Their grandmother Glendora recalled for him the name of the retired trooper who Clyne and Gabe had discovered had witnessed Jovanna removed from the scene of the accident. It was a reminder that none of them needed. Clay spoke to Kino briefly and thought he'd never sounded so happy. Clay pushed down the tiny stirring of jealousy at his brother's good fortune as his thoughts went to Izzie Nosie again.

On Wednesday, Clay picked up several strays off one of the tribal highways. There was a council meeting tonight, and Izzie was on the agenda. He mentally reviewed all the information Clyne had given him on procedure for the meeting. He went home, showered, ate some leftovers and rattled around the empty place until he could stand it no longer. Then he headed to the meeting early.

Izzie was already there. She came to greet him, her eyes darting nervously about as she licked her lips. He took her hand and kissed her on the cheek in hello, then felt he had overstepped when her face flushed, and she glanced around to see if anyone had noticed them. Was she still ashamed to be seen with him? Had she accepted his help merely out of desperation?

That thought made his insides ache. If it were true, it just might kill him. All he could think of since Monday was Izzie. He was determined to do his best to help her. But was that all she wanted from him—his help?

Clay and Izzie waited in the hall until the doors to the chamber opened at six thirty and then walked side by side down the center aisle. The council table was empty, but the room was not. Filling the front row on the left side sat the tribes' general livestock board, including their clerk. On the aisle was Franklin Soto. Donner filled the next two seats, lounging back in his chair with legs crossed at the ankle and his fingers laced over his generous stomach. Pizarro sat next to Donner and leaned over to speak to him. Clay would have loved to know what he was up to since he had the authority to choose which of the tribe's pastures were subject to re-nourishment. On the end, closest to the wall, huddled Victor Bustros, Pizarro's clerk, who dealt with the mountains of paperwork necessary to hold and sell cattle including the lists of all the individual brands. Though not actually on the board, he attended all meetings with the livestock board. Bustos had his head inclined to listen to-ward Pizarro and Donner but was not engaged in the conversation.

Clay chose the front row as well, taking a seat closest to the general livestock board. The choice was intentional and reminded Clay of the two sides of a legal battle, prosecution and defense. Donner noticed him and sat forward to greet him, but as Izzie moved past Clay and sat to his right, Donner's smile morphed to a grim line joined with a hard stare. His boss glanced from Clay to Izzie and then back to Clay, giving him a wither-ing look at Clay's decision to ignore his warning.

Over the next ten minutes, members of all three tribal communities filtered in. Finally, about fif-teen minutes after the meeting was scheduled to begin, the tribe's council appeared. They always met in private sessions prior to the public meeting. Clyne said that was where the real business was done.

Clay knew them all—three women and three men. With Council Chairman Ralph Siqueria still absent, there was the possibility of a tied vote on any issue. Clay watched his brother take his seat behind a nameplate and smiled; the pride still rose every time he saw Clyne there among the tribe's leadership. Their mom would have been so happy. Arnold Tessay, the longest-serving member of the council, sat beside Clay. Their clerk, Martha Juniper, a broad woman notable for her fry bread and her owlish glasses, asked them to rise and honor both the American flag and the tribal flag. That done, the tribe's acting chairman, Dennis Faden, called the meeting to order.

Clay waited for their turn. When the matter of the permits was raised, Izzie asked for the explanation, just as Clyne had advised. No one seemed to know why that land was scheduled for renourishment. Pizarro, who was in charge of such matters, stated that it was a rotation, and this land was overdue.

Izzie replied that the land had not been overgrazed and then asked for an extension to allow for the council to inspect the property in question.

Tessay said they didn't have time to check

every cow pasture, and that was why they had a general livestock coordinator. Clyne proposed that he and Pizarro have a look at the pasture in question and report back to the council. The council voted to delay the question, and the motion passed with Tessay and Faden against, Cosen, and the three remaining council members for. Izzie had her stay. Her cattle could remain until the council met again in one week's time.

Clay's delight was diminished when he and Izzie stood to leave and walked past Gabe, who still wore his uniform and looked less than pleased to see him here.

They made it out into the parking lot. The weather girl had been right. The sky was clear and glistening with silver stars. He tugged his denim coat closed against the chill as he halted beside Izzie's truck. For some reason, his brain chose that moment to remind him of the empty house waiting for his return and the privacy he would have if he managed to convince Izzie to join him.

"Well, you have a few more days," said Clay.

"Thank you for all your help. I never would have known what to do, procedure and all. And Clyne calling for a motion, I know that was you, too." She lifted up on her toes and kissed him on the cheek.

"Isn't that your neighbor?" Clay asked and drew her farther into the shadows.

It was, and he was deep in conversation with Clay's boss. Izzie strained to hear anything of the exchange between them.

"Did you know Floyd offered to buy my cattle?" she said.

"You said he asked you out."

"Yes. But yesterday he offered to *buy* me out. Right after my permits notice arrived. It was like he knew."

"Could be. News travels fast." Clay looked back at the man in question, gesturing with his hands as he spoke to Donner. "He got that kind of money?"

"No, which is why he gave me a low-ball offer. Take them off my hands, he said. You'd have to be a fool to take that kind of deal."

"Or desperate," said Clay. "Maybe with the troubles you've been having, he figured you might be wanting to get out of the cattle business."

"Victor Bustros called me, too. This morning. Said he'd heard about my troubles and offered to auction my herd."

Bustros worked under Pizarro. But as brand inspector one of his duties was to oversee the tribe's auctions.

"I didn't know."

"They're like sharks smelling blood."

All round them came the sound of cars and trucks starting. Headlights flashed on, and vehicles pulled out from the gravel lot on to the highway. Izzie lingered, hands shoved in her pockets. She wanted another kiss, and another and another. She tried to remember why that was such a bad idea, but all she could recall was how right it felt to be in Clay's arms.

"You want to go get something to eat?" he asked.

She didn't want food. The want she had was much deeper, more primal. Izzie wanted the pressing of flesh to flesh. His heart beating beside hers. She wanted the heat and the wetness and the friction. But she didn't want to be the subject of gossip. She knew the viciousness of the wagging tongues around here. It was a small community in a small reservation. Clay was living proof that people didn't forgive or forget a misstep. She had to guard her reputation. She was a businesswoman with a mother and two brothers to provide for. She should walk away.

Instead, she asked, "Isn't Kino away on his honeymoon?"

Clay's brow quirked and he went very still.

Had she really just said that? She didn't know who was more surprised, she or Clay.

"Yes," he said, not making the offer that she wanted.

"So you're alone out there." She couldn't be less subtle than that.

"I am. You like to come over for…"

She gave him a wicked smile and nodded.

"Okay. Two trucks or one?"

She didn't want to leave her truck out here where anyone could see it and make assumptions. Besides, someone would surely see Clay driving her back here in the morning.

"I'll follow you."

"Great." But his expression didn't say great. The tightness at his mouth and the lack of enthusiasm in his tone told her he'd pegged this for what it was, a quick hook-up that no one else needed to know about.

He opened the door to her truck and gently caressed her arm as she swept inside.

Izzie had ten long minutes to reconsider. But she didn't. She just sat in the parking lot for a full minute, giving Clay a head start before she drove after him. When she came to the turn that would take her home, she didn't take it. Instead she pressed her foot down, accelerating into the curve as the anticipation built. How many years had she dreamed of spending the night in Clay Cosen's bed?

"Just one night," she whispered, giving herself permission.

She saw his taillights and forced herself to slow, giving him a few minutes to prepare for her arrival. She lingered in the driveway and stared up at the stars sparkling above. Dividing the sky from the earth stood the dark silhouette of the Black Mountain. Her people had lived in the place so long it was a part of them and they a part of it. She felt it then, the beating pulse of the earth beneath her joining in sacred ceremony with the beat of her heart.

The door to his house opened, and Clay filled the frame, dark before the light within.

"Izzie?" he called.

And she went to him, entering his home as he swept aside to make room for her passing, before he closed the door behind her.

He took her coat and ushered her in to the living room. She glanced at a very tempting couch that looked long enough for them to stretch out. They sat on the soft sofa, she by the armrest, he on the center cushion. She wondered if her mother would notice her absence. She often came in from livestock meetings to find the lights out and her mother's bedroom door shut. It was her mother's way of reminding Izzie that she did not like the cattle business or the cattle her husband had left to his daughter.

Izzie turned toward Clay, admiring his familiar, handsome face and knowing they were also strangers, separated now by years and experience.

"Can I get you a drink?" he asked.

She shook her head and pivoted toward him. She lifted a hand to caress the hard blade of a jawbone. Izzie met the intense gaze that gave Clay the air of danger. Clay sat still, as Izzie explored his face with her fingertips, becoming familiar with the man he now was. She slid closer and looped her arms around him, lacing her fingers behind his neck. She sighed in satisfaction, recalling all the prayers that Clay would be hers.

And now he would be, and she wondered why, in all that time, she'd never once asked to keep him and still keep the peace in her home. Her father had warned that this man would cost her everything. Had he been right?

She had made a promise to her father to run the business, but did that mean she had to live like a nun? For a moment she let herself imagine what it would be like to have Clay, not just for tonight, but every night. She wanted that. But if life had taught her one lesson, it was that you did not usually get what you wanted. You had to choose carefully.

His phone rang and they both jumped. He

glanced down and saw it was Clyne. He turned the screen so she could see, and she nodded. His brother might have more news.

"Hey," said Clay.

"Hey. I'm not sure what's up with those grazing permits, but Tessay was adamant that we not interfere with Pizarro's decisions. Undermining him, he said. He said we've never questioned him before, and it set a bad precedent."

"All true," said Clay.

Izzie wondered if he should tell Clyne she could hear him.

"But there was something about it. Didn't feel right. You coming over to Grandma's tonight? We can talk some more."

He grimaced. "No. I'm beat."

A hesitation. Had his brother made a guess as to what was really occupying him?

"Tomorrow, then," said Clyne at last.

"Sure. Tomorrow."

Clyne disconnected, and Clay set the phone on the coffee table, turning his attention back to her. She gave him a smile that she hoped was full of sensual promise. Tonight, she would pretend that nothing would separate them.

Izzie stood and held out a hand to him.

He reached, clasping tight. He remained seated, looking up at her with what she thought might be hope. His hand gripped hers more tightly as if he was afraid she might let go. The taut lines at his mouth showed that he was unsure what she was doing. Did he think she might leave him now? She wouldn't. She wouldn't leave him unless dragged from his arms. All those wasted years haunted her, and so did her need to always do absolutely everything that was expected. Acting, not doing what was right for her, but what was right for everyone else. Well, not tonight. Tonight was about what was right for her and for Clay.

"Izzie?" he asked.

"Show me your bedroom, Clay."

He was on his feet so fast, she startled back a step. A moment later he swept her up in his solid arms, leaving the living room behind. He was bigger and stronger now. His face had changed, too, becoming more angular and his eyes showing a wariness that she had only glimpsed when he was a teenager. It came from his father back then. Now it came from being betrayed. Izzie vowed to never betray his trust.

She laughed as he hoisted her with no effort and fairly flew down the hall that led to a room cast in shadow. She could see all that was important: the large bed and headboard. He laid her down upon the soft comforter, and she was enveloped by his masculine scent. It was heady as any alcohol, and in moments she was drunk with passion.

She lifted a leg, and he tugged off her boot and socks. Then he repeated the procedure on the other leg. He abandoned her for the time it took to remove his own boots and socks.

He rested a knee upon the bed, and she realized with a thrill of dread and excitement how big his body was compared to hers. She reached, and he knelt beside her. She reclined on the pillows, and he braced himself as if he meant to do a series of push-ups. Instead he lowered himself inch by delicious inch until he pressed her down to the bedding. Their mouths met, and her flesh tingled. She threaded her hands in his thick hair and tugged him closer. He held his weight off her, his chest just skimming against her breasts as he swayed side to side in the most deliciously sensual move. The gentle friction drove her crazy, and she surged up to meet him, pressing her breasts to the arousing hard surface of his chest. He rolled to his back and carried her with him. Her legs now straddled his denim-sheathed thighs, and her belly came in contact with the evidence of his need for her. The thrill of anticipation beat inside her with her thrumming heart. He deepened the kiss, their tongues now sliding one against the other. But she needed to feel his skin against hers, so she pulled back. Her eyes were adjusting to the light filtering in from the hallway now, and she could see the tension in his jaw as he waited for her. This was Clay. The boy she had loved and the man she desired.

His breathing was heavy. She sat up, shifting so she straddled his middle and came down on his hips. He sucked in a breath and released it in a hiss. If she didn't know better, she'd think she had hurt him. But the pain he felt was just like hers, need and longing mixed with desire.

"Oh, Bella," he said. "I've dreamed of this so many times."

She smiled and grasped at the fabric at her waist, clasping the hem of the turquoise button-up blouse she wore and dragging it over her head. Beneath she wore her best bra, which was low-cut but not extremely revealing. This was just a plain white lace B-cup that she filled. But it didn't seem to matter because Clay now stared up at her in wonder, as if she were the most erotic thing he had ever seen.

"You're beautiful," he whispered as his hands slipped up to encircle her waist. His grip slackened, and his fingers danced down her back, sending a delicious tingle over her skin. Finally, he cradled her backside, still unfortunately clad in her best black jeans. He tugged the two of them into closer contact and she thrilled as he rose up to kiss the bare skin at her shoulder. She sat straddling his waist, letting her head loll back as he showered hot, wet kisses on her neck, his tongue and teeth arousing her flesh.

She stopped him only to drag off his plaid flannel shirt and the white T-shirt he wore beneath. It was like Christmas morning, she thought, exploring his square shoulders, broad chest and muscular back. Her fingers roamed over taut rippling muscle and velvety skin. The pads of her fingers grazed over warm flesh that dimpled under her touch. She smile in triumph, relishing the reaction of her touch, but her lips fell open with a groan of pleasure as his mouth found her breasts, soaking the lace over one hard nipple and then the next.

They were so good together and it frightened her.

But it didn't stop her, not as she eased out of her jeans. Not as she unfastened his. She wasn't turning back. Tomorrow would be soon enough to deal with the fallout of this decision. Tonight was her chance to make the biggest, most wonderful mistake of her life.

Chapter Sixteen

Clay couldn't believe this was happening.

As he kicked off his jeans, he could hear the voice of doubt reminding him that she had not been honest with Martin. She had told him that she had gone out with Martin in order to be with Clay. Martin had told a different story. One that had just about killed him.

But that was in the past. Yet another past he'd never really been able to put behind him, even now when Izzie was here in his bedroom stripping out of her jeans and panties and bra. He followed suit, dragging off his remaining clothing and tossing them away. He wanted her desperately, but not so desperately that he did not stop in stunned silence at her beauty. She knelt before him on the bed, naked and mysterious as the night. Her breasts were larger than the last time he'd touched them, the nipples the same soft rosy brown and tight now with excitement. Her flat stomach and muscular thighs showed the results of many hours of physical labor. But now she had the narrow waist and flaring hips of a woman. He stared at the glossy black thatch of hair, and his mouth went dry. Gone forever was the thin, playful girl he had known. Izzie was now entirely woman in body and spirit.

Medicine Root Woman, the shaman had named her at her Sunrise Ceremony. Grounded, powerful and somehow momentarily his.

When he lifted his gaze it was to find her surveying his body. What changes did she see?

Their gazes met, and they shared a smile as they reached in unison for each other. She pressed against him, and his body twitched and jumped with need.

He dragged the fastening from her hair, releasing the coiled rope from its neat, functional bun at the back of her head. Her glossy, deep brown hair unwound until it lay across one shoulder in a twist. He finger-combed the silky strands over her shoulder and down her back, restoring the black curtain that he had always loved. Then he captured her, bringing her head to his chest, allowing him to inhale the scent of her hair. Still sage, he realized. She inched closer until her sex met his.

He stilled, closing his eyes for a moment to thank God for his good fortune. He'd lost her for so long. Now he prayed for a new beginning.

That she was no longer ashamed of him. In this moment, he realized why it was so important to keep his job and earn back the respect he had lost on that day long ago. It was for Izzie. He wanted to be the man she deserved. To make her proud.

Clay kissed her mouth, and Izzie let him take her weight, trusting him with her body. He lay her back on the pillows, tasting her as he explored the recesses of her mouth. Then he moved down her throat to kiss her perfect breasts. His reward was the soft moans of pleasure that escaped her parted lips as he continued to kiss and stroke.

He didn't know why Izzie was giving him this second chance, but he planned to do everything he could to please her. He dipped lower. Izzie's cries became more frantic, and she reached out with desperate greedy hands, whispering for him to take her. He drew back. He wanted her more than almost anything. But not so much that he would take advantage of the best thing in his life.

"Bella, are you sure?"

She opened her eyes. Her lips were swollen with his kisses, and her need called to him louder than any siren.

"Yes. Now, Clay. I need you." She didn't lie there waiting but took hold of what she wanted.

Now *his* breath came in a ragged pant. "Let me get a condom."

"I'm using birth control."

"No condom?"

She shook her head. "I want to feel you."

Wasn't that the ultimate show of faith? She trusted him, deep down and wholeheartedly. Clay felt so happy he thought he might cry. But he didn't. Instead he shifted between her legs and eased down inside her. It was that first slow, silken glide that met with resistance. He glanced up at her as a question formed in his brain, but she lifted up, and he slid deeper. Isabella stilled and then began to move. He wanted to go slow, to savor this first time, but the pleasure and the need to move won over his good intentions, and he drove hard to match the pace she set. He relished the change in her breathing and the arching of her back as she reached her pleasure. He followed a moment later. He dropped down upon Isabella and let her finish him. As the mind-blowing sensations rocketed through him, he dragged her against him, wishing he never had to let go.

As his body relaxed, his mind re-engaged, and he thought to wonder as she lay nestling in his arms, why, after all these years, had she picked this night to take what he had offered her so many times before? His grandmother, who was a very wise woman, had once told him that a woman's heart is not so easy to read as a man's. A man loves or hates. But a woman can do both at the same time. She might use her body to hurt a man or use a man or love a man. The trick, of course, was to know one from the other. That memory disturbed him and kept him from sleep. There was something else that bothered him, but he could not quite remember what. Finally, he realized what it was that had tried to break through his thoughts, back when he had no thoughts but finishing what Izzie had started.

Martin had lied to him, not once, but twice. Clay knew that because, despite all the tales Martin had told him, until tonight, Izzie had been a virgin.

Clay stroked her glossy hair and listened to her soft breathing. Finally he dozed and woke when Izzie slipped from his arms. He rose on an elbow and followed her with his eyes as she disappeared into his bathroom. Then he flicked on the bedside lamp. The evidence of his suspicion was there on his skin. Isabella's innocence and Martin's lie. He wondered why he'd believed Martin when he said he'd taken her again and again. And why he had believed Martin when he'd said he wanted to grab a pop from that store.

Now, at least, Clay understood why Martin had risked his neck to steal the money to take a frightened little Mexican girl. He felt stupid all over again.

He listened to the water run and then stop. The

door opened, and Izzie paused, naked and beautiful in the soft glow of his reading lamp.

"Why didn't you tell me?" he asked.

She blushed and lowered her chin before looking at him through a forest of thick dark lashes. "Because I was afraid you'd say no."

As if he could ever refuse Bella anything.

"Are you all right?"

She nodded, but she didn't stand tall as she usually did, and there was a tentativeness about her that he didn't recognize.

"Are you sorry?" he asked and then gritted his teeth against her answer.

Her chin came up. "No. I'm not. I've always wanted it to be you. I just never expected it to take so long."

He lifted the covers. "Come here."

She did, sliding in beside him and nestling face-to-face on his pillows. He draped a leg over her and dragged her closer, then he rolled on to his back. It was hard, because he wanted her again. But he'd wait. There would be time, he thought. She rolled toward him, and one of her legs glided across his thighs. He sighed at the sweetness of having her in his arms. Clay drew slow circles over her back and closed his eyes, forcing down the desire. Had he really thought that taking Izzie would get her out of his system? She was like the drug he could not shake. The

Mountain, Clay knew, responsible for keeping track of every brand for every Black Mountain rancher and all the brands for the tribe members who kept a cow or two in the tribe's communal herd. But he worked with Boone Pizarro.

"This stinks."

"Maybe. Anyway, Victor went at sunup. Carol gave permission for him to have a look. He found she had too many cattle, and so he checked the brands. Some of her cattle had been recently branded."

"That's not illegal."

"They'd been branded over a previous brand."

"Whose?"

"Those belonging to Floyd Patch."

Clay struggled to find an explanation. "*Patch* was the one missing cattle?"

"Yeah."

"And they assumed Izzie took them?"

"There's been a lot of activity up there. Logical to check the neighbors. She'd been driving cattle, possible that some of his got out and mixed with hers. They didn't think she stole them. Floyd's fences aren't well maintained. We pick up his cattle all the time. In fact I would have bet my paycheck they were his cows out on the highway that day."

"But they were Izzie's cattle."

Clay rocked back as if Gabe had punched him

in the gut. He glanced back at the cruiser to see Izzie staring at him. Clay's gut churned as the disbelief gave way to a far worse feeling, the feeling of being used yet again.

"It would explain why she has been registering record numbers of calves year after year. She could have just been collecting Patch's strays."

"But wouldn't he notice the loss of cattle?"

"Apparently he did. This time, anyway." Gabe glanced back at the cruiser, checking on his prisoner.

"This is a mistake."

"You sure about that?" asked Gabe.

"She's not a thief."

"You said the same thing about Martin."

His brother's words struck him like a second punch to the gut. Was it possible? Had Izzie been so desperate to make ends meet that she'd do something like this?

"Why? Why would she?"

"To cover her mother's debts. She's been paying them off. I checked. It's a lot, Clay."

He thought he might throw up.

"Would explain the cut fences. It would be a good place to bring in the stolen calves."

"You don't have any evidence to support that." Why was he defending her?

Gabe shrugged. "Just starting to gather evidence now."

les over his chest at the ache that was deeper than skin and muscle and bone. He thought about Gabe coming back for him. Charging him with some damn thing, like conspiracy or failure to report a crime, which was about the same charge as before and showed he didn't have an ounce of sense when it came to judging peoples' intentions.

How was it he could read sign but couldn't read the truth in a person's words?

"Not again," he said.

Time to cut his losses and protect what little reputation he had left. Clay returned to the house to retrieve his phone. He would call Izzie's mother, as he had promised, and then put Isabella Nosie and her troubles behind him.

He might just talk to Mr. Donner and then drive on up to South Dakota for a long weekend. See if he could help Kino and Lea find that case manager and locate their sister. That's where his allegiance should be, with his family. Hadn't he once told Kino the same, when his little brother had been hell-bent on finding their father's killer, instead of helping Gabe and Clyne in their search for Jovanna? Now he was guilty of the same thing.

Clay located his phone and saw three messages. The first two were from Gabe alerting him that he was coming to his house to arrest Izzie. Clay now thought to wonder how Gabe knew that Izzie was with him and realized that he'd likely gone to Izzie's place first and then made a logical guess. That meant that Izzie's mom already knew her daughter was in trouble and where she had spent the night. The third message was from Kino, telling him the good news. His brother sounded jubilant, and the happiness in his voice only made Clay feel worse.

Clay pushed the hair from his face and sank into a seat at the kitchen table, contacting something soft. He pivoted to find Izzie's coat still draped across the back of the chair. He dragged it from its place and hugged the sheepskin sheath to his chest, breathing in the scent of leather, the horses she loved and sacred sage.

His words came in Apache squeezing through his tightening vocal cords. "Ah, Medicine Root Woman. Did you use me, too?"

CLAY DIDN'T ACTUALLY remember showering or getting dressed. But he did remember making coffee, because he burned his hand on the old percolator pot he used on the stove.

His phone rang, and he checked the caller ID. It was police headquarters. He stared, knowing that his brother would call from his mobile if he needed to speak to Clay. So that meant this was Izzie calling him from jail.

He stood looking at his phone until it stopped

ringing. Then he waited. She didn't leave a message. Clay stared at the missed-call notice. He just couldn't deal with her problems anymore.

He turned away. Took two steps into the kitchen, gathered his truck keys and stopped. Clay remembered making that call. He remembered when all his friends vanished and the only ones who stuck by him were his family. Who did Izzie have? A judgmental, demanding mother? Two kid brothers? She needed him to believe her, and he'd done just what everyone once did to him, assumed she was lying. Clay redialed the number and was told that Izzie was in processing, and she had already used her phone call. She'd called her mother. But he knew that she had called him first, and he hadn't been there for her.

Truth from lies. That's what it all boiled down to. Did Clay believe Izzie or did he believe the evidence of the rebranded cattle found among Izzie's quarantined herd?

Clay slipped his phone in his pocket and gripped his truck keys in his fist. Izzie was being set up. He felt it. And he should have believed her when Gabe escorted her out. She wasn't using him like his old dearly departed friend, Martin. She was asking for help from a friend.

During his eighteen months away, he'd learned to climb and navigate. He'd learned to meditate and to engage in trust activities. And he'd trusted the other guys there with his life. But he'd never trusted anyone with his heart. Until now.

If Izzie was playing him, then he'd find out the hard way, just like he did everything else. He was not leaving Izzie on her own in jail. He couldn't. Because he still loved her.

Clay called his boss but got Veronica. He wasn't coming in today. He had to help a friend.

Then he headed over to the police station in Black Mountain.

There he was told to go to work as he couldn't see her until after processing. Clay knew what that meant, remembered every detail, right down to the gray-green chipping paint on the bars of the holding cell. Clay hung his head in shame as he recalled how he had just stood there as his brother drove Izzie to jail. What had he been thinking?

He couldn't get to her, so he went to work, not to the livestock offices.

His brother had enough evidence to make an arrest. His brother was a very good judge of character, but when he erred it was on the side of being too cautious. He didn't leap before he looked. That was why he was who he was and why Clay was about to take the biggest leap of his life.

Because he was going to prove her innocent and get her out of jail.

The place to begin was where this had started,

Izzie's land. Clay headed back over to Izzie's pastures to see if there was anything he had missed at the original sight. He hadn't, but he did find something newer by several days, a portion of the fence that had been cut and expertly mended. He also found tire tracks and boot tracks, two sets. He called Gabe who came over.

"I'll photograph them," said Gabe. "What do you reckon?"

"Only reason to break a fence is to let something out or in." Clay pointed at the ground. "See?"

Gabe squatted and looked, but Clay thought his brother didn't really see.

"Cattle tracks?" said Gabe.

"No," said Clay. "Those are too small for cattle. Have to be calves. Old enough to be weaned, from the size. And they are coming in, not out."

Gabe stood and dusted the sand off his knee.

"I'm going to talk to Patch," said Clay.

"No, you are not. You're not interfering with my investigation, or I'll arrest you, too."

Gabe must have seen Clay's face redden, or maybe it was the intake of breath. Anyway, Gabe removed his hat and ran his thumb over the brim, silent for a moment. Then he faced his younger brother.

"I'm sorry, Clay. But you need to let me do my job."

Clay wanted to tell him to do it then. Or yell at

Gabe that he was trying to help him. But he just managed to hold his tongue. Clay stared at Gabe, who rested his hands on his hips and scowled.

"What do you want me to do?" asked Gabe.

"Come with me to see Patch. I'm sure these are the kind of boots he wears."

"Lots of folks have construction boots."

"I'll match them."

"What do you think he did, exactly?"

Clay studied the ground. "Someone chased Izzie's cows out through the cut a few days ago. She'll prove it when she gets her hearing. Here someone has added cattle to her herd. Gabe, someone is messing with her."

Gabe nodded, agreeing with that. "This cut is newer. See how the tracks are dried all round? Yesterday."

Gabe's mouth went grim. "You think someone rebranded those cows with Izzie's brand and then set them loose in her pasture."

"Yes."

Gabe's eyes shifted down the hillside. "How did they get her brand?"

Clay shook his head, unsure.

"Let's go have a talk with Floyd," said Gabe.

Clay grinned, feeling the first ray of hope finally breaking through the clouds that had surrounded him all day.

Gabe nodded, and the two drove down the hill

to Floyd's place. They got out of their respective vehicles together and headed to Floyd's home, where they were met by his sister, Celia Batista. She lived there with her husband, Ron, who worked the place with Floyd. Celia had a round face, dark eyes squeezed by her pudgy cheeks and a body that seemed a series of ever-increasing rings of fat. She wore a shapeless flowered shirt, knit slacks and flip-flops pressed flat from overuse. Celia directed them to the barn.

"There's soft sand out here in the drive. Get him out here so I can see his tracks," said Clay.

"Wait here." Gabe left him and returned a few minutes later chatting with Floyd. "Just need you to sign a complaint," said his brother, motioning to the truck.

Floyd's smile dropped when he saw Clay. "What's he doing here?"

"Asked him to come on out to read some sign."

Floyd's stride lost its confident swing. He seemed less willing to follow Gabe out on to the dirt drive. Gabe looked back, waiting.

"Something wrong?" he asked.

Floyd was sweating now, but he shook his head and followed Gabe to his cruiser. Clay made a careful study of their passing and then nodded to Gabe.

Gabe asked Floyd to wait and retraced his

steps, being careful not to walk over the tracks they had made.

"You sure?" he asked Clay.

"Positive."

"Well, now." Gabe returned to Floyd who sputtered and demanded to know what was going on, so Gabe told him.

Celia hurried out in the yard, but her bluster vanished when she saw her brother's face turn ashen.

"So," said Gabe to Floyd, "you going to tell me how you got a hold of Isabella's brand here or at the station?"

Floyd said nothing. Ron and his wife exchanged a long look. His wife shook her head, her hands now clasped stiffly over the most prominent roll of her belly.

"Floyd, I've got you for cutting fences and tampering with Izzie's herd. I've got your tracks leading right into her fence line. And I suspect you're the one who rebranded your own cattle and you're the one who let some of her herd out on the highway last week. So someone would notice the rebranding."

Floyd was rubbing his neck as if he were a chiropractor.

"I hope that's the worst of it," said Gabe, sounding conspiratorial now, as if showing serious concern over Floyd's welfare. "But there's things going on here, Floyd. Serious federal crimes."

"Don't say anything, Floyd," said his sister.

"Hush up." He turned to Gabe. "I got the branding iron from Eli Beach. He helps her out, and sometimes he works over here with Ron and me. I said I wished I could get her to sell out, and he suggested rebranding."

"Eli suggested it?"

"Yeah." Floyd's hand dropped back to his side.

"Where is he?"

"Not here."

"Well, that was real helpful of him," said Gabe. "You pay him?"

"No."

"Strike you as strange that a man would do something like that for free?"

Floyd hiked up his jeans. "Well, it does when I hear you say it."

Clay couldn't keep the smile from forming on his face. Izzie was innocent.

"Why'd you want her cattle?" asked Gabe.

"Not her cattle, really. I wanted those permits. Her land is better."

Because Izzie's dad had busted his hump clearing trees instead of complaining about it like Floyd, thought Clay.

"If she sold, she wouldn't need them," Patch went on, his voice now whiny as a mosquito.

"Isn't right that she gets those permits year after year. She can't hardly keep that place running, even with help."

Especially with help from a man who was stealing her branding iron, thought Clay.

"Your brother-in-law in on this?"

"Floyd," screeched his sister. Then, seeing Floyd hesitate, she hopped right in. "He didn't know."

"Except he drove the four-wheeler through her pasture," added Floyd.

Gabe had a heck of a time keeping Celia from beating her brother, and Clay found he was enjoying himself for the first time in days. Gabe got Celia off Floyd but had to threaten to arrest her before she calmed down. Gabe lost his hat in the scuffle, which Clay retrieved and returned. Gabe replaced it on his head and turned back to Patch.

"You know anything about those meth cooks up there?"

Floyd lifted both hands in a gesture of rejection. "I surely do not."

Gabe leaned in toward Floyd who cowered back.

"If I find out you are helping the traffickers or the cooks," said Gabe, "I swear I will fight for federal prosecution, Floyd, unless you come clean right now."

The color drained from Floyd's face, and he

pressed both hands over his heart as if fearful it would stop. It was one thing to be caught rebranding. But it was quite another to face a federal charge for narcotics, a drug-related offense that the tribe would most likely turn over to the district attorney to be tried by the State of Arizona.

"I don't know nothing about the crystal meth cooking. I swear."

Clay's smile vanished. If Floyd was telling the truth, then Izzie's troubles were far from over.

Chapter Eighteen

Izzie waited in the cell all morning, expecting her mother to come bail her out. But her mother didn't come. Her mom wouldn't like idle talk about her daughter being mixed up in something like rebranding. Was her mother's reputation more important to her than her daughter?

When Izzie had paced herself out, she settled on the narrow stainless steel bench that was bolted to the wall and wondered if this would be her bed tonight.

As soon as she stopped moving, her mind dragged her right back to the look on Clay's face when Gabe put her in the squad car. It hadn't been indignation or worry or even disbelief. She would have loved to see disbelief on his face, because that would have meant that he thought she was innocent, that some mistake had been made.

No, what she had seen on his face was shock as he reached the conclusion that she had betrayed him, just as Martin had done. A moment later his jaw had turned hard as setting concrete.

But she had not used him. She had called him from the station to tell him so. He had ignored her phone call. Cut her loose. Decided already that she was guilty.

It didn't matter that she hadn't done it. What mattered was that he could believe she would. He didn't trust her. Oh, he'd slept with her. He might even have loved her once. But he just wasn't willing to take the kind of risk involved with trusting her with his whole heart.

She could just smack Martin Ethelbah right in the teeth, if he wasn't already dead. Gone but not forgotten, she realized. Never forgotten because his ghost still haunted Clay Cosen. Maybe he always would.

She didn't recall Martin's exact last words to her before she broke it off, but it was something to the effect that if she wouldn't have sex with him, he would find a girl who would.

She cradled her head in her hands and wondered why, with all her problems, the thing that cut her straight across her heart was Clay's face when she drove away.

He'd let her call go to voice mail. Izzie sagged and then straightened as she remembered his call to her after *his* arrest. How he left a message telling her he was innocent and begging her to believe him. She'd never picked up and never called back. Now he had done the same thing. The shame hit her deep. What a horrible thing, to be denied the chance to explain. Yet she had done that to him for *six years*. Perhaps she deserved to be sitting in this cell, if for no other reason than it made her realize what she had done to him. No. To them.

As the morning turned toward midday, Izzie began to wonder who was setting her up.

"Izzie?"

She startled at the sound of her name, rolling off the tongue and ringing with a familiarity that made her tingle and the hairs on her arms lift straight up. Clay stood before her, his hands on the bars as if he were the one in the cage.

He glanced up and around.

"Still looks the same," he said and then gave her a gentle smile.

A ray of hope entered her heart.

"Clay?" She rose. "I didn't do it, Clay."

She went to him, expecting him to pull back. But he didn't. Instead he extended his arms through the bars and took hold of both her hands, dragging her to him until they were separated only by the vertical steel.

"I know," he said.

"How?"

"Because I know you, Isabella Nosie. I know

you promised your dad to look after that place for his sons. I know you'd do just about anything to keep the ranch going, but just about is a far cry from anything."

She beamed at him. He believed her.

"Your brother thinks I'm guilty."

"Naw. He just had enough evidence to make an arrest. But I've been doing some investigating myself." Clay held up a ring of keys.

She gasped and stepped back. "Clay, you cannot break me out of here."

"See," he said. "Still the good girl. Won't even leave the jail when the door swings open."

He tried a few keys before finding the right one and then grinned.

"Gabe asked me to bring you out. He's dropping the charges."

She peered through of the open door and down the hall to the police offices in the tribal headquarters.

"Why?" she asked.

"Because you're not guilty and because we found who is."

He took her arm and guided her out past the series of desks and into the office of the chief of police. Clay positioned them between the chairs before Gabe's desk and the bank of glass windows looking out to small desk-filled room that was the tribal police station.

"Thought you'd like to see this." Clay pointed, and Izzie watched from behind the clear glass as Floyd Patch and their shared ranch hand, Eli Beach, were marched past them toward the booking area.

"Eli?"

"He took your brand and gave it to Patch. Might have been his idea. Patch rebranded some of his own weaned calves and then he and Ron broke into your pasture again to add them into your herd."

"And they were spotted in impoundment."

"Yes, as you left. Bustros, the brand inspector, noticed it. I believe Gabe is looking into that. Trying to sort that out. Matching stories up. Looking for inconsistencies. He's really good at that—details, I mean. Scary good."

The tears Izzie had swallowed down all morning erupted like a thundercloud, and she wept. Clay gathered her in.

"Shh, now. Everything will be all right."

When she finished choking and sputtering, she asked Clay why they had done this to her.

"Permits," he said. "Floyd wants them, and he can't have them unless you give them up."

"What about the pasture renourishment? I still have the permits, but I won't be able to graze my cattle there for over a year."

"Something stinks about that, too. Gabe is looking into that, as well."

She stepped back and tilted her head to study his face. His smile was a little too fixed and did not reach his eyes, which she knew sparkled with his smile and danced when he laughed. His smile faltered.

"It's not over, is it?"

"No."

"What should we do now?"

"I'm not sure."

Gabe arrived, looking rushed and overworked as usual.

"He's got a strong alibi for the seventh." Gabe glanced to Izzie. "Hello, Izzie. I see he figured out which key." He extended his hand to Clay, who gave him a large ring of keys. "Patch says the veterinarian was over at his place in the morning of the shooting. He recalls seeing the police vehicles go by. If it checks out, then he might not be tied up in the drugs."

"Can we go?" asked Clay.

"Sure. I might have more information tonight if you want to come to Grandmother's for supper. And Friday, Luke will be there."

Luke Forrest, the war hero, FBI agent who folks around here either idolized or despised. He'd gotten off the Rez. He'd made good. But he was a Fed and that was something that Apache just didn't do.

How had Clay's uncle done it? Clay's father, Luke's older half brother, had been a drug trafficker who had been murdered in his kitchen, and Forrest had ended up enforcing the law against such things. Strange world, she thought.

"Can I bring Izzie?" Clay asked.

She could tell from the long pause that Gabe didn't like that idea.

"Tonight?" Gabe asked, clarifying.

The brothers exchanged a long look that Izzie could not read. Finally Gabe nodded and then went back to the interrogation room. She watched him go.

"Ah, Clay? I don't think I'm coming over for supper. I've got things to do." The auction was tonight. She had cattle to sell and a fine to pay.

Clay's shoulders sagged, and his mouth went tight. The muscles at his jaw twitched.

"Sure."

She'd hurt him. She knew it. She just didn't know how.

"Come on. I'll drive you back to my place."

"Your place?"

"To get your truck."

She felt her face flush, as she realized what was happening. Clay thought she didn't want to be seen with him. And why wouldn't he? There had been a time when that was true. But that was before he helped her prepare to face the tribal council. Before he figured out what was happening on her land. Before he came and got her out of jail. Before she spent the best night of her life in his bed.

"Clay, I think you have the wrong idea about this. I'm not ashamed to be seen with you."

His brow arched and he cast her a hard look.

"Sure. I understand."

But he didn't. And she didn't think telling him otherwise would do a thing but waste her breath. Since Clay's return to the Rez, so many people had turned their backs on him. And she had been no different. The shame of that now ate into her bones like cancer.

Clay was exactly the kind of man she had always wanted, and now she needed to be the kind of woman he deserved.

Chapter Nineteen

Clay took Izzie to his place, and she kissed his cheek goodbye. He didn't try to hold her or to kiss her back. He had freed her from jail. And she said she wasn't ashamed of him. But there were six years that said otherwise. As Clay saw it, the only way to know whether Izzie was really willing to accept him was to solve her troubles and then see if she still wanted to become a part of his life.

Until then, he would keep his head down and his eyes open. Clay headed inside alone and found the place too quiet, but it was only Thursday, and Kino wouldn't be back until next Sunday at the earliest. He spent the evening haplessly moping and packing some of his belongings. He opted to sleep on the couch to avoid the memories of Izzie in his bed, but they just followed him out to the living room. He slept badly and was up and to work so early on Friday morning that he found the office was still locked. The morning chill chased him back to his truck, where he was when Donner rolled in twenty minutes later. He gave Clay an odd look as he parked beside him.

The two men exited their respective vehicles simultaneously and headed toward the office together. Donner's face was inscrutable, and Clay slowed to a stop at the door as dread hit the lining of his stomach. Hadn't Veronica told Donner that Clay was taking a personal day yesterday?

Clay thought of the time he'd been away with Kino and the days he'd missed all or part of the day while helping Izzie.

"I can make up the hours," offered Clay.

Donner made no answer.

"I'm fired. Aren't I?" asked Clay.

That made his boss's brows lift in surprise. "No, you're not. Gabe was here yesterday. He wanted to ask me some questions. He wouldn't tell me exactly what was happening, but I gather that you figured out how Isabella's cattle got loose and how they got rebranded. That's good work."

"You're not firing me?"

"Clay, you are one of my best men. I wanted to offer you my help. I'm not the tracker you are, but I'm a good shot and good with cattle. Plus, Isabella's father was a friend of mine. So if you need a man, call me."

Clay blinked in surprise.

"I also wanted to tell you that if you think

Izzie's pastures don't need renourishment, then you should look to Pizarro. He's the one who makes that call, and until this happened, I'd have said he was an honest man. But when I questioned him, he told me that I should mind my own business. That's no answer."

"Really?"

"He did. So I thought you might want to send Gabe to see him."

Clay looked at his boss with new eyes. "Why are you doing this?"

"Same reason as you. Someone is messing with Izzie Nosie, and I don't like it."

The two shook hands, and it felt different somehow, as if he and Donner were equals. Clay left the office a few minutes later with orders to move the branded yearlings and cows to a new pasture. First he called Gabe and told him about Donner's suspicions. Then he went to work. It wasn't enough work to keep his mind from Izzie. It was hard not to call her. He checked his phone often to find no message, texts or missed calls. Finally, he gave up and called Gabe again, asking for an update, but Gabe told him if he wanted information, he should come to supper at their grandmother's that night.

At quitting time Roger asked if Clay wanted to go grab something to eat, but Clay turned him down in favor of dinner at his grandmother's table.

Clyne had sent him a text that their uncle Luke had arrived. Clay wanted to find out if his visit was official business or social, so he headed over to his grandmother's, stopping only long enough at his place to shower off the dust and grime earned from a hard day's work.

At his grandmother's, Clay was greeted to the mouthwatering aroma of a roast in the oven. The beef, potatoes and onions all combined to make Clay's salivary glands fire and his stomach rumble. He closed the front door, and Clyne called a greeting from the dining room. He found both his eldest brother and his father's half brother sitting at his grandmother's table before the remains of a pumpkin pie. Luke rose to hug Clay and slap him on the back.

When they drew apart, Luke took a long look at him.

"More good news about your sister," he said.

Clay's gaze flicked to Clyne.

"I don't think he knows yet."

"Oh," said Luke. "Well, let me be the first to tell you. Kino spoke to the case manager and found out that Jovanna was in a foster home on the Sweetgrass Reservation until 2008. When it shut down, she was moved off the Rez with a foster family."

Clay's gaze flicked to Clyne. He knew how strongly Clyne felt about Native American children being removed from Indian homes and raised by white families. Clyne's expression was stormy, as expected.

"Is she still in that foster home?" asked Clay, as the hope began to rise in him, becoming real. Kino was getting close. His little brother might not be able to read sign as well as he could, but he sure could do investigative work. The only one better was Gabe.

"We don't know yet. He's on his way to Rapid City to find out."

"Well, that's great." He looked about the kitchen. "Where's Grandma?"

Clyne chuckled. "She's off to talk to her sisters. Planning an invitation list for the Sunrise Ceremony. I think she's going to invite the entire tribe. We'll need every bit of the cow Nosie is going to give you."

Luke knew about that? What else did he know?

"So," said Clyne, "what's up?"

"Gabe said that he got tipped about the re-branding from Victor Bustros," said Clay.

"The livestock brand inspector?" asked Luke.

"Yeah," said Clyne.

"Bustros works for Pizarro," added Clay.

Clyne picked up the story. "And at the council meeting, last week's, not this week's, Pizarro—

he's the general livestock coordinator—listed Izzie's land for renourishment with several others. I've looked at her pastures since. They're healthy. Tessay seemed in a hurry to call the question, and he had the votes, four to two. It's a routine matter. Motion passed. I never knew until afterward that none of the four who voted to renourish had seen the pasture beforehand, which is unusual."

"Why unusual?" asked Luke.

"Most times one or two of the council members go to look at the overgrazed pastures."

"Isn't that Pizarro's job?" asked Luke.

Clyne shrugged. "Never popular, closing a pasture. Sometimes he wants the backup."

"But not this time," said Luke.

"No."

"So you've got Patch, guilty of rebranding, releasing another rancher's cattle and actually slipping his cattle in with hers. And the second problem of the permits," said Luke. "And that little trouble with the gunfire, dead cattle and the evidence of someone cooking crystal meth on Izzie's soon-to-be-renourished land."

"Also the improved road," said Clay.

"Right," said his brother. "I checked into that. And we have no order for road improvement from the tribe. Yet there it is on Nosie's upper pasture, big as life."

"The kind of road you would need to bring in big trailers?" asked Luke.

"Yes," said Clay. "But why is it there?"

"I can handle that one," said Luke. "We have intel that the cartels are moving the ingredients for cooking crystal meth over the border. Because of what Gabe has told us, we believe they are setting up on the reservations to avoid federal jurisdiction. According to our contacts in Mexico, we have got a lot of agricultural precursor unaccounted for, and they would need that to make the drugs. And that area, where Izzie lives, is just inside the reservation boundaries but in a spot way off the beaten track. The road in and out is easy to defend, because you can see traffic coming from both directions."

"Gabe should hear this," said Clay.

"He has," Luke said. "What you can't see is someone riding up on them from the lower pasture."

"Like you and Izzie did," said Clyne.

"Also, since that spot is secluded and close to the main highway, it would be easy to move product. Good place to store product, too, except for the problem of the rancher and her cattle. So they need to get Izzie off that land."

"Who?" asked Clay.

"That's what we aim to find out," said Luke.

"Are you going to the council?" Clay asked.

"Nope."

"I thought you needed permission to bring in the FBI or any outside agency on to the Rez," said Clay.

"That's so," said Clyne.

"But I can come back home visiting anytime I want," said Luke, "because I'm still a member of this tribe."

"This is an unofficial visit. That way there is no paperwork."

Clay turned to his brother. "But word will get out that Luke is here, and everybody knows he's with the FBI."

"We don't need much of a head start," said Clyne.

Clay put it together. "You think someone on the council is involved."

Clyne shrugged. "Gabe says the bad guys always know when the Feds are around."

"And where they will be," added Luke. "So while I'm here, I might ride along with Gabe or come chat with Clyne. Unofficially. I was hoping you might bring me over to Izzie's for a visit."

"I could do that."

"Great."

"What about your partner?"

"She's close. In case I need her."

"She ever been on the reservation?"

"Not this one. She worked up in South Dakota. Covered the same territory where Kino is now."

"She Indian?" asked Clay.

Luke laughed, and he and Clyne exchanged a look of confusion.

"She's white. Very, very white. And serious." He whistled. "She has a daughter, so that proves she's human, but other than that…well, all business. She's a widow and a mom, so…" He shrugged.

"That's tough," said Clyne.

"What happened to him?" asked Clay.

"She never said. Doesn't talk about it. Anyway, she worked in South Dakota and then in California and now down here with me."

Clyne jumped in. "Gabe met her. Said she's so white she's really pink. Got blond hair the color of corn pollen and blue eyes. He said she looks like she's from Sweden or something."

Clay knew that Clyne, with his traditional values and aesthetics, had never even dated a white woman. Though he had many white friends. Political friends, activist friends. Clyne never seemed to be off duty.

"Norway. Her ancestors, I guess. Anyway, they didn't hire her for her looks," said Luke. "She's tough as rawhide. Officially, she's trout fishing. I also suggested she visit Pinyon Fort and the museum for a little culture."

"You should bring her and her daughter over for supper," said Clyne. "Grandma will want to meet them."

"Her girl is staying with her mom, I think. And I don't want Cassidy connected to me. Not yet. Far as anyone knows, she's a tourist."

Before Clyne could respond, his phone rang and he excused himself. Luke and Clay settled at his grandmother's table and Luke helped himself to another generous slice of pie.

"She know you ate that pie?" asked Clay.

"Not yet, but I plan to be gone before she finds out." Luke grinned.

Clay debated waiting for the roast, but opted for the last slice of pie, destroying the evidence.

"So, how are you doing with Donner?" asked Luke.

"It's a good job, and I'm grateful to you for getting it for me."

Luke waved away the thanks. "I just got him to give you a shot. You're the one who's kept it. I admire you, Clay."

Clay lowered his fork. "Me?" He couldn't keep the surprise from his voice. His uncle was a shining example of what a man could make of himself. And he'd done it all on his own.

"Yes. You. *You* stayed. *You* faced your past, and you are making a name for yourself. Folks speak highly of your honesty and work ethic."

That was just nonsense. When folks spoke of him, it wasn't to mention his work ethic.

Clay pushed away the remains of the pie and studied his uncle. He looked like his father in many ways. Same shape to his face. Same easy smile. Same peaked hairline. Only Luke's hair was bristling short, and his father had always worn double braids.

"My work ethic?" He snorted. "I wouldn't have had a chance at that position if not for you. That job means everything to me, and I know how lucky I am to have it."

Luke's smile dropped, and he sat back in his chair. "Everyone needs help sometimes. Like the help you've been giving your girl."

"She's not *my* girl." Though he was thinking that was what he really wanted her to be.

"My mistake," said Luke.

Clay held back his frustration but made a poor job of it, judging from his uncle's curious expression.

"What?"

"You've never made a mistake," said Clay.

"*Everyone* makes mistakes."

Clay cast him an impatient look and then dropped his gaze. Luke was his elder. Even if he were not, he was also family and due respect.

Luke patted his arm, and Clay met his gaze.

Something had changed, but he didn't know exactly what.

"Okay," said Luke, "I think it's time I came clean about a few things. You're family, and so I think you have a right to know just what kind of help I had."

Clay placed his fork on the empty plate and directed his attention to his uncle. What had he done? Stolen loose change off their father's dresser?

"You know I wanted to join the US Marines. You might even know how *much* I wanted it. But when I was seventeen, I got drunk at the quarry, and your dad didn't want me to drive. He was drunk, too. Not as bad as me, but pretty drunk. I wouldn't give him the keys to the truck. *My* truck. So I drove." Luke's hand settled on his own neck. "I drove right into an embankment. Six months from graduation and enlistment papers all signed and I crashed my truck. Your dad was nineteen. He'd already been expelled from school. You know what he did that night?"

Clay leaned in, waiting, hoping this wasn't another story of his father's failings. It was a long list. But this was before Clay was born. Before Clyne was even born. Before his mom and dad were married, before the drug charges.

"He switched places with me. Told me he was

driving. Told me not to say otherwise. And you know what? I did. That sound like a hero move to you?"

Clay sat back as understanding came and, with it, all the implications.

"Your dad was a dropout and a troublemaker, but he was still my big brother. It wasn't the first time he hauled me out of a jam. Like Clyne does in your family. I wasn't perfect, despite appearances. My brother, your father, told me to shut up when the police came. I did that, too. Your dad was arrested for DWI, and I joined the US Marines and shipped out. You know the rest. Except, if he didn't have that prior, then two years later, when he was on his honeymoon with your mom, his DWI would have been a first offense. He wouldn't have gone to prison. He wouldn't have met the gang members and begun driving for the cartel. You see? All that might not have happened. And yet, he never said a word about it after. Never told a soul. When I tried to thank him, he told me I could thank him by taking care of his sons. So I've tried. I didn't just plead your case because it was the right thing. I did it because I know that a nineteen-year-old makes stupid mistakes and that teenagers shouldn't be treated like adults. You deserved a second chance, Clay. And you've earned it many times over. I only wish…"

He let go of his own neck and clutched his coffee mug. "I wish your dad had been given a second chance, too."

Luke sipped his coffee. Clay sat in silence as he realized that the uncle he'd always idolized was human. Flawed. Did that mean they all were? Mistakes. Punishment. Redemption.

When was it enough? He glanced at Clyne, standing in the hall, speaking on the phone. What mistakes had he made in Iraq or on the road with the rodeo circuit? Was the difference between him and his perfect older brother only the difference of getting caught?

"Thank you, Uncle," Clay said formally. "For telling me this."

Luke gave his nephew's cheek a pat, as if Clay were still just a boy.

"So who do you think is setting Nosie up?" said Luke.

Clay brought his attention back to Izzie's problems. "Arnold Tessay, one of the tribal council members, pushed for the vote that revoked Izzie's grazing permits. Victor Bustros is Tessay's man, and he is the one who first noticed the rebranding. Eli Beach is a part-time ranch hand who stole Izzie's brand. My boss oversees impounding cattle and sits on the general livestock council with Boone Pizarro. Pizarro also ordered the renourishment. I think her neighbor only wanted her permits, but who knows?"

Clay wondered if he was not also under suspicion.

"That all?"

"All I know."

"Long list," said his uncle. "You in touch with your old friend Rubin Fox?"

"I went to see him when I suspected meth cooks."

"What did he say?"

"To stay the hell away from him and also to stay away from Izzie."

"What do you think he meant by that?"

"At the time, I thought he was implying that she was involved, but now I think he might have meant that she was in the middle of some big trouble."

"So he cares enough about you or about Izzie to give you a warning. Surprising."

"Yeah. He's involved with the drug trade. Just like his dad. He's hooked into…"

"Distribution. Yeah. We know him. His dad was a minor player with a small box truck. Ran drugs from the border with Frasco Dosela. Worked with your dad, too, actually."

Clay had not known that. But he knew Frasco because he was the father of the woman Gabe planned to marry. Now Frasco was in federal prison and Gabe was still single.

"Someone else is moving product now. Not sure who. Rubin is protected by his Native status and by the fact that he never leaves the Rez. I'm sure Rubin has got prospects and probably information. Will he talk to you?"

"I doubt it."

"Well, try, anyway. See if he'll meet you somewhere, somewhere public. I'll speak with my friend Donner. I already put Cassidy on Tessay."

"Cassidy?"

"My partner."

"Your partner's name is Cassidy, like Butch Cassidy?"

"That's her first name. Last name is Walker."

"Cassidy Walker? Sounds like the name of a Texas Ranger."

Luke gave a chuckle. "Yeah, well, I told you that she's here trout fishing? Guess who I got for her guide?"

Clay shrugged, giving up without a try.

Luke smiled. "Tessay's son, Matt. And she's very persuasive, charming when she's not being a bad-ass."

Gabe arrived, in uniform and in a rush, as usual. He motioned to Luke, and the two stepped out into the backyard and closed the door behind them.

His grandmother came in, and Clay helped her set the table, then kept her company as she removed the roast from the oven to cool down. Clyne returned from his phone call and glanced out the back window at Luke and Gabe but gave them their privacy. When the food was ready, his grandmother broke up the meeting, calling Gabe and Luke to the table. It was nice to share a meal with his family. His uncle took Kino's usual place, and the table was filled again. After supper, Clay bid the group farewell and kissed his grandmother good-night. Then he returned to the dark, empty house.

He thought of Izzie, wished he could call her and take her out. But though she had shared his bed, she was not willing to share a cup of coffee with him, at least not in public.

Clay understood. Funny that he'd never appreciated how important a man's reputation was until it was lost.

On Saturday morning, Clay called Rubin and got his voice mail. He left a message and then continued packing for his move back into his grandmother's home. When he stripped the bed, he lifted his sheets to his nose. Izzie's scent hung faintly to the linens. By the time he had the laundry packed, his phone rang. He fumbled in his pocket for it, hoping it was Izzie. He stared at the caller's name.

Rubin Fox.

He answered.

"Rubin?"

"You call?"

"I need to talk to you."

There was a momentary pause. "Come on, then."

"Where?"

"You know where."

Clay's heart sank. He had let Rubin set the location, and his uncle had told him to meet his former friend only in a public place.

"Well? You coming?"

"Yes," said Clay.

"See you in twenty, coz."

The phone went dead. Only now did he think to wonder why Rubin had agreed to meet.

The Wolf Den. The hangout of the Wolf Posse and the last place in the Rez Clay should go. He grabbed his keys.

Chapter Twenty

Clay headed to Rubin's place of business, a house on the eastern side of the Rez community called Fort Pinyon, after the stronghold of the same name. Past the museum and the fort lay an area closed to all but Apache tribal members. Inside that area was an unofficial community that folks called Wolf Canyon, but the only wolves there were members of the Apache gang, the Wolf Posse. They operated here, far from the tribal headquarters and close to the most sacred ground outside of Black Mountain itself.

Most of the tribe avoided Wolf Canyon except when looking for trouble or a score. There was always plenty of traffic. The homes were boxy, colorless and old like everywhere on the Rez. He glanced at the peeling paint on stucco walls, dry rotting wood, sagging gutters and windows repaired with packing tape. Everything looked like a postcard sent to those philanthropists back East asking for money for the Indian College fund.

He pulled up before the wolf den, a washed-out beige stucco ranch, notable because of its position at the end of the road and because the windows were secured with metal bars. For a moment Clay thought of the irony of Rubin leaving prison and then creating one here. He noticed Rubin's black pickup. His vehicle was dusty but too new for a man who supposedly existed on government subsidies. Beside it was a beige four-door sedan with a tribal license plate. That made Clay frown. Who was the tribal official visiting the wolf den?

Clay left his truck, looking past the two vehicles to posse headquarters. The door, designed to keep unwanted visitors out, stood wide-open. The small hairs lifted on Clay's neck, and he reached for his phone to call Gabe. Then he remembered what his brother would say, what he always said. *You're not an investigator. Wait for the police.*

But Rubin wouldn't leave that door open. Never. That meant Rubin was in trouble. Clay shouldn't care but found he still did. Once Rubin had been a friend. Clay had thought that their friendship had died long ago of neglect. Did he owe Rubin anything? He didn't know, but he did know he wasn't waiting for the police.

Clay stepped out of his truck and onto the tufted mounds of yellow grass that no one bothered to mow. The silence was chilling. Where was his posse, the gang of men whom Rubin always said had his back?

Clay wished he carried a gun and then remembered Gabe saying the best way to get shot was to carry a gun. He thought walking into the wolf den unannounced and unescorted was also an excellent way to get shot.

Clay brought up Gabe's number on his phone and let his thumb hover near the green call button. Then he entered the house. The light was muted because of the brown packing paper someone had secured with gray duct tape over every window. What happened in this house was private, from the sale of drugs to the plans to move shipments around the reservation. As far as Clay knew, Rubin had never moved up to trafficking off the reservation, and his uncle said the same. Had Rubin learned his lesson from his father's mistakes? Staying on the reservation reduced his chances of facing federal prosecution. After all, he was Apache and so not subject to the laws of the US government, as long as he stayed here, with his people, and as long as his people didn't turn him over to the Feds—again.

Clay called a hello and was met with silence. There was a rifle propped against the wall between the entrance and living room.

Clay hugged the wall, the dread making his stomach drop. He glanced at the firearm but left it where it was.

"Rubin?" Clay said and was met with no reply. "It's Clay."

He peered through the entrance toward the living room. His gaze swept the room before snapping to the body that lay between the living room and the adjoining room beyond. Two legs poking out and arms spread wide as if the man was falling backward into cool water. The legs were clad in jeans and the two feet sheathed in the expensive unlaced sneakers Rubin favored.

Clay stepped through the door, already smelling the blood. Rubin laid face up, eyes open, mouth open and hat still on his head. But his head seemed to have settled too far onto the floor. And behind him on the carpet was a large crimson stain that Clay knew must be blood. Lots of blood. Clay stared as his skin rose into gooseflesh. He didn't remember backing out of the room but found himself standing in the room's entrance, one foot in the hallway as if the sensible part of him was preparing to run.

Apaches did not associate with the dead. It was the worst kind of bad luck. Rubin's ghost might follow him. But Clay was also a Christian, and a Christian did not leave a friend's body unattended. Still, Clay wished he could be like his ancestors and burn the entire place to the ground before striking camp and moving away forever.

He caught movement from the dining room,

and then the sound of a pistol shot pinged. Clay ducked back into the hallway, crouching behind the wall, knowing from the bullet hole that now pierced the Sheetrock above him that the wall offered no protection.

He pushed the call button on his phone. Dropped the phone in his breast pocket and then reached for the rifle.

"Don't shoot. It's Clay Cosen."

"Clay?"

He knew the voice but could not place it.

"Who's that?" he asked.

"Arnold Tessay. Don't shoot."

Arnold Tessay? What was the councilman doing here? Was that his vehicle? Clay tried to recall if Tessay was related to Rubin. Apache family trees were complicated. It wasn't hard to trace everyone back to a mutual relation. Then Clay's brain reengaged. Tessay had fought hard against Izzie's permits. He'd insisted on the quarantine of her herd. And he was cousin to Rubin's father.

"Did you shoot Rubin?" asked Clay.

"I'm putting down my gun. Come out."

Clay thought he wouldn't do that just yet. He hoped Gabe had picked up but couldn't check without releasing one hand from the rifle.

"I called Gabe. He's on his way." He said that loud enough for his brother to hear, if he'd picked up. "Why are you here, Mr. Tessay?"

"If you're staying, I'm going."

There was a thump, like something heavy hitting the bare floor. A moment later Clay heard the back door open and close. He took a look into the room, where Rubin's body remained. But now there was a pistol just beyond his outstretched right hand as if he'd died with it in his grip. Clay turned and saw the bullet hole in the wall and a new kind of terror welled.

Through the open front door, Clay saw movement in the yard. He rushed to the entrance. Arnold stood beside the sedan.

Clay stared in confusion. "You can't leave the scene of a crime."

"Hell, boy. I can do anything I want. I'm a tribal councilman. And you're a convicted criminal who just killed a man."

"I didn't kill Rubin."

"Well, that rifle in your hand says different. It's the murder weapon, and it's got your prints all over it. The pistol shot came from Rubin's gun. Unfortunately, he missed. Won't matter. You didn't." Tessay removed the work gloves he wore. "Have fun in prison."

Clay stared in horror at the rifle as Tessay laughed.

The councillor slid behind the wheel. "Two drug dealers. They'll believe the worst and think they're better off with you both gone. Be hard on your grandma, of course. But she's got three good boys. That's something."

Clay couldn't even speak. His numb fingers extended, and the rifle clattered to the ground.

Tessay pointed at the rifle at Clay's feet. "See now, I thought you would have shot me. That's why I took out the bullets."

"You made Rubin call me. Lie to me. Get me over here."

"Well, he works for me. Worked. And it's no lie. Izzie is in trouble. Big trouble. Cartel is on the way to her place now. We tried to get her off that land. Lord knows, I tried. If it hadn't been for that stupid, greedy Floyd Patch, she never would have been up there in that pasture counting her herd, nosing around. I got to go." He started the engine.

"Why? Why take Izzie's land?"

"It's the perfect spot for a mobile meth lab. I'll have it under renourishment for three years or so. That gives the cartel boys time to cook product without worrying about the Feds. As tribal council member, I'm alerted to any joint initiative with the federal authorities. Gives me time to warn them and them time to move. Scourge of our community—drugs. But very lucrative."

Clay now understood why Gabe could never find the meth labs they knew were operating on the Rez.

"You betrayed your people."

Arnold snorted. "Like hell. The cartel don't sell here. They sell to the whites. I'm just doing my part to help them destroy themselves. Think of it as a modern version of the Ghost Dance, a way to make them all disappear." He closed the door and placed an elbow on the lip of the open window.

Clay took a step in his direction and met with the snub-nosed barrel of a pistol.

"I'll tell them what happened here."

Arnold laughed. "Great. You do that."

"They won't believe you," said Clay, his stomach twisting tighter then the cinch around a bronco's belly. They *would* believe him. Every word.

Tessay grinned like a man holding a winning hand. "Wait for your brother and find out who he believes. You or the evidence. Or you can run after your girlfriend. You might get there in time to get shot, too. If I were you, I'd be heading to Mexico. Give me a call from there. I'll hook you up as a driver, like I did for your dad."

That information staggered Clay a step. He regained his balance as Tessay backed out and drove away. Before the dust had settled, Clay heard Gabe's voice, far away and tiny. He drew out his phone.

"Did you hear that?" Clay asked.

"Some. Just you, really. Stay there."

Clay was already running to his truck. "You've got to get to Izzie. She's in trouble."

"Stay there. I'm sending units to her now."

"I'll meet them." He was closer to Izzie's place than police headquarters. Closer than home where Gabe had been. He'd get there first. He had to.

CLAY MADE IT to Izzie's place in record time. He found the house empty, and so he headed to the barn to find Max Reyes sitting on a roll of hay, his head in his hands as if he were crying. Max was a hand for hire, but since Eli had been providing her branding irons to Patch, she was shorthanded.

"Where is she?" asked Clay.

Max Reyes startled and shot to his feet, reaching for the closest weapon, which turned out to be a flat shovel used to clean stalls. His hands trembled, and his eyes were wide.

"I couldn't stop them. They would have killed me, too."

The idea that Izzie was already gone washed over him like cold rain. Clay stepped forward, and Max swung the shovel. Clay caught it and wrenched it from his hands. An instant later he had Max off his feet and pressed to the wall of Biscuit's stall. Clay's gaze flashed from Max to the place where her horse should have been.

"Where is she?"

"They called me. Told me to tell her that her

cattle was wandering on the road again up by the drug cook site. An accident, they said. It would look like an accident."

"How long ago?"

"I don't know."

Clay banged him up against the stall, and his hat fell off.

"Fifteen minutes, maybe."

"Why didn't she take you?"

"I told her I'd follow in the truck."

Clay dropped Max, who sprawled on the dirty ground. Clay glanced around. He needed a horse. A fast horse. He made his choice and was lifting the saddle when Max came at him. He should have stayed down. Clay dodged the punch and countered with one of his own, hitting him square in the forehead. Max's eyes rolled up, and he fell so hard that Clay felt the impact of his head hitting the dirt-packed floor through the soles of his boots.

He took one more moment to look at Max, who was breathing but unconscious.

"I ought to kill you," muttered Clay. Instead, he tied Max like a roped calf, with all four appendages locked behind him. He had to get to Izzie.

Clay lifted his phone to warn her and saw he had no service. Izzie had no service, either. Not until she got up to that improved road and he hoped like crazy that she wasn't there yet. The urgency pressed him on.

Clay gathered from her barn what he could in a hurry. Rope, saddle, blanket, machete that Izzie used for cutting bailing twine. He always carried a lighter, knife and phone. And from his truck he grabbed his saddlebags that held his fishing kit, hooks, line, sinkers and some hunting gear. As he mounted up he wondered if having a gun would just get him killed quicker or keep Izzie alive. For the first time since returning from the elite Native American tracking unit of Immigration and Customs, known as the Shadow Wolves, he wished he carried a rifle in his car like every other Apache he knew. But everyone he knew wasn't a convicted criminal. Everyone he knew didn't understand the difference between a conviction with a deadly weapon and a conviction with none. The difference between him and Rubin Fox.

He had no idea how many they'd sent to kill Izzie or how they intended to make it look like an accident. But the images of her in different deadly encounters swam before him as he pressed his heels to the powerful mustang she called Red Rocket and hoped the gelding lived up to his name.

He rode to the upper pasture, hugging the fence line. Praying he wasn't too late.

Chapter Twenty-One

Izzie kept glancing over her shoulder. Max should have been up here by now, and the longer he took the more unsettled she became. She used to be at home here, on this land, in the pasture. And if not happy, at least content with her purpose. She used to look forward to fulfilling her promise to her father, turning over the ranch to her brothers and finally beginning a life of her own. But gradually, year by year, her dreams and goals had begun to disappear. She was nearly twenty-five now. Was it already too late?

Back when she had received her Apache name, Medicine Root Woman, at the Sunrise Ceremony, she had known what she wanted to become. Then her father died. And she learned that she was good with cattle. Managed to increase her herd. But she didn't like cattle. They were stupid and needy and fearful. She liked horses. Thought she might raise them one day. In her heart, in the places she didn't admit aloud, she wanted to be a large animal vet. Schooling took time and it took money. Neither of which she had. Her time was not her own. The money belonged to her brothers, or it would, someday.

What would happen then, when the boys could do a man's work and she gave them what was theirs? What would she do then?

Her eye tracked movement, always looking for gopher holes that could break a horse's leg and harm the cattle that got themselves in every manner of predicament despite her best efforts to give them safe pastures. She spotted the large black SUV the moment it appeared from the road that led up the mountain. The size, clean exterior and shiny newness made the vehicle stand out. As it approached she noticed the tinted windows, and the hairs on her neck lifted. It looked like what she imagined might be used in the president's motorcade. But here, on Apache land, such trucks meant only one thing: drug business.

She glanced about for the nearest cover and found the rocky slope and wooded area that led to the improved road. As she turned she saw Clay, charging up the hill on her chestnut mustang, Red Rocket. He was waving her toward the woods. His speed and the wild gestures only liquefied her unease into a cold breaking wave of panic.

She didn't look back toward the fence or the approaching vehicle but tore across the open ground at a full gallop, scattering the cattle that separated her from cover. The first sound she heard over the cattle's mooing and snorts was a single pop. Her heart, already pounding in her chest, seemed to stop.

She'd been around enough firearms to recognize the sound of a rifle shot. She flattened to her horse's back as more shots sounded. It wasn't clear if they were shooting at her or at Clay or both. She glanced to him, seeing Clay motion her down and then dropping out of sight himself. Now all that was visible of Clay Cosen was his leg swung over the saddle as he gripped the cantle between his thigh and calf muscles. His mount, Rocket, continued on, familiar with this unusual mode of riding.

They used to ride like this as children, imagining themselves in a time when her people wore red headbands marking them as army scouts and warriors.

Izzie swung herself from the saddle, looping her elbow over the saddle horn and her knee over the cantle. The cattle surrounded her as Biscuit continued at a lope through the herd that swallowed them up.

Beyond the fence the pop, pop, pop of gunfire continued. She hoped they didn't hit her cattle. Glancing forward, she saw the trees and the exposed gray rock. She and Clay broke from the herd together, separated by only fifty feet.

"Who are they?" she shouted.

"Cartel. Here to kill you."

Her fingers still gripped the reins, but they were numb now and bloodless.

Why, she wondered. Why did they want her dead? The land. The permits. It had to be.

Their horses climbed the steep outcropping of rock, Izzie first, Clay just behind on the narrow animal trail. Another series of shots sounded, and Biscuit stumbled, dropping to her forelegs.

Izzie cried out as her weight shifted, and she fell beside her horse. She was on her feet and tugging the reins, her gaze fixing on the stream of blood now flowing from her mount's shoulder.

"Oh, Biscuit!" she cried.

"Leave her!" shouted Clay. He landed beside her, still gripping Rocket's reins, and tugged Izzie to her feet.

"No," she howled, but he propelled her along, using Rocket's large body as a shield between her and danger. They reached the cover of the series of large boulders and pines. Bullets sparked off the rock, sending sharp shards of stone flying. Only when all three of them had reached cover did Clay release her arm. Rocket's barrel heaved, and foam fell from his mouth as the gelding recovered from the hard ride up the steep hill.

Izzie dropped to her knees, also panting as she struggled to fight the urge to vomit.

Clay was pressed to one of the boulders, peering back at the shooter's position.

"Three I can see," he said. "Can't tell how many still in the car. Two, maybe."

Izzie swallowed and then crawled next to him, gathering Rocket's reins. Behind them, Biscuit gained her feet and was limping painfully up the incline after them.

"I have to get her."

Clay reached out and grabbed Izzie's shoulder.

"They aren't shooting at Biscuit. You go out there, and she'll get hit again."

Izzie dropped to her seat as tears burned from her eyes and flowed down her cheeks in splashes of hot pain. Biscuit didn't deserve this.

She glanced at her mare's wound and the blood, then up to Biscuit's head. There was no blood coming from her horse's nose. It looked like the bullet had hit muscle and bone. Not her lung. Izzie rubbed her own chest in sympathy. Then her eyes went to the rifle sheathed and tied to the front of her saddle, mostly for killing snakes and gophers.

"The gun."

Clay glanced back to Biscuit. Then without a word he leaped up and exploded over the ground, running. He grabbed the rifle from the sheath tied to her saddle, and Izzie heard the sound of more gunfire. Clay threw himself down, and Izzie sat with both hands clutching her throat. Had they shot him or was he taking cover?

Clay began moving, using the downed logs and low rocks as he crept back up the incline. Izzie wished she could return fire as the gunshots continued, pinging off the rock. It was the longest thirty feet she had ever seen. But as Clay made his heroic approach, Izzie realized something. She was a fool.

All these years she had let her need to be the perfect daughter ruin her chance at the one good thing in her life, her love for Clay Cosen. She loved him, irrationally and with all her heart, and if that made certain members of this tribe turn up their noses, then so be it. She didn't need them. She didn't need her spotless reputation or her mother's approval, either. She needed Clay.

And she needed them both to get out of this alive.

Clay fell in beside her, breathing heavily. She threw herself into his arms, and he hugged her with his one free arm.

"Thank you for coming for me."

"Thank me when we get out of here," he said. He moved to rise, and she let him go. She'd always turned to him in times of trouble, and he had always been there for her. Izzie felt the creeping unease as the truth crawled over her skin like spiders. She had used him. Was using him right now. This wasn't his fight. It was hers. Clay deserved better than a fair-weather friend. And that was exactly what she had been. When he'd turned to her, she had turned her back.

"I'm so sorry," she said as the tears came harder.

Clay squeezed her hand. "Izzie, I need you to pull it together."

"I was so mean to you."

"What?"

"I didn't even come see you when you came home."

He looked at her as if she'd gone mad. "Izzie, there are guys shooting at us. Can we talk about this later?"

She sniffed. Nodded and wiped her nose on her sleeve.

Clay peered over the rise.

"What are they doing? Are they coming?"

"No. One got in the car."

Leaving? They were leaving.

"Thank God," she whispered.

Clay continued to watch. "Where are the other two?"

Izzie peered over the rock and watched the SUV as it climbed the road and then turned.

"Where are they going?"

"Going to pull in above us. At least that is what I'd do."

Izzie's heart hammered. They were now trapped between an open pasture and the road.

"Gabe is coming," said Clay. But his gaze was flicking about as he took in their position and the enemy who was now capturing the higher ground.

Izzie looked toward the road. "They're waiting for us to leave this cover."

Clay looked back across the open pasture. "Can't go that way. They'd pick us off. But we gotta move. Now."

Chapter Twenty-Two

"Stay low," Clay said as he grabbed Rocket's reins and hoisted Izzie up on the horse. They left the animal trail and made for deeper cover. Behind them, the men on the road disappeared into the woods.

"Should I shoot at them?" she asked.

"No. Save the bullets. Come on."

They continued on. When the branches encroached, she slipped from the saddle, following beside Rocket. A moment later the shooting resumed from the direction of the road as their attackers below caught glimpses of them through the pinyons. One bullet splintered the bark of a tree trunk just inches above where Izzie had placed her hand. But she kept going, following Clay deeper into the thicket. Clay knew the woods. He knew how to track and trap. But he had always been the hunter. Now they were the hunted.

From here she could see the gravel road just

above them. Was he trying to get past it, to the woods beyond? It would make sense not to be trapped between the men behind and the road ahead. But it was too late.

"I can see them," she whispered, pointing. "Coming up the road."

"Can you still climb, Izzie?"

She nodded. Clay boosted her up the tree trunk and then instructed her to throw his lariat over a branch above her. She did as instructed, and before she had even thrown the rope, Clay had shinnied up a nearby sapling and used his weight to bring the top of the trunk to the ground. It was a game they used to play, bending saplings for the ride down. But she knew the other purpose of such a setup because her father had taught her. A snare, a big one, used to capture a large animal. Clay secured the bowed tree and then moved rapidly on the ground, fashioning a large noose that he hid in the branches of the shrubs on either side of the path. One side of the loop lay on the ground, but the other was a few inches off the forest floor. The noose was so artfully camouflaged that she thought she might walk right into it even knowing where it encircled the path. He secured the other end of the rope to the bowed branches he had staked and covered the line with debris. As she watched, the snare vanished. She hoped the cartel members were city boys.

"Come down," he whispered, and she scurried back to him. They moved on. Clay stopped three more times, using his fishing line to run invisible threads across the path and again to make a lasso of wire line, which he placed partially in the stream. This one he set with several hooks. Above them, the men neared.

"Can't we just hide? Wait for Gabe?"

Clay shook his head. "I don't want my brother shot."

Had she actually just suggested they crawl away and hide while his brother face the danger directed at her? Izzie's cheeks flushed hot as she decided it was past time for her to stop running from trouble and expecting everyone else to face down her problems.

"You're right. What can I do?"

He gave her instructions. It was dangerous. They'd have to separate. She needed to lure them but keep them from getting a good shot at her.

"Don't use the gun unless you have to." He handed it to her. "That will give away your position and lead the ones on the road to you."

"Okay." She turned to go, but Clay stopped her by capturing her by the arm.

"Izzie, I have to tell you something else. Tessay's working with them."

"Why are you telling me this now?" And then she knew. If it came to it, Clay would give his life up for hers, and he wanted her to know what he knew.

"Oh, no, you don't. Don't you die on me, Clay Cosen."

He grinned and saluted. "Yes, ma'am."

A moment later the killers' arrival was punctuated by the sound of gravel crunching under tires followed by car doors slamming.

"You remember what I said?" Clay asked. "Use the horse to startle them and take cover."

"What if they shoot Rocket?" she asked, the anticipation and worry broiling inside her.

"What if they kill you instead? Who will look after your brothers then? Rocket?"

Izzie straightened her spine and prepared to do what must be done. She gripped Rocket's reins in one hand and the rifle in the other. She nodded her readiness. Clay clasped her chin between his thumb and curved index finger. She leaned in and gave him a kiss. Their mouths met greedily. Then he left her, running fast in the opposite direction.

Izzie led Rocket to the place where he could be seen from the trail, a living decoy should the men get past Clay's traps. Then she dropped the gelding's reins. Rocket was a good horse and knew that a dropped rein meant to stay put. She tied a lead line on the side of his bridle and walked as far from the animal path as the line allowed, taking cover behind a cluster of rocks. As she habit he would do anything to fill. Izzie's fingers kneaded his chest like a cat, and she closed her eyes.

Clay reached and switched off the bedside lamp. There in the darkness, with her heart beating slow and her breathing gentle, he held her as she drifted to sleep. It took him some time, because of the images of Izzie beneath him and the images of what else he'd like to do with her. But finally he slipped into slumber that was broken by the faraway bleating of his phone. He glanced at the clock and saw it was already 6:56 in the morning. He had to get to work, and Izzie needed to get home. He opened his eyes and stretched. His phone was on Do Not Disturb from midnight to seven, so only those on his favorites list would get through. All others had to call twice to get his phone to ring.

Izzie blinked up at him. Her hair was tousled and her skin glowing with health. She slept on her stomach and had kicked off the covers, he realized, giving him a good long look at the slope of her back and the lovely round curve of her buttocks. When his gaze returned to her face, it was to find her grinning that wicked smile she'd cast him last night.

"Good morning," he said and kissed her brow.

She pushed the hair off her face and lifted up

on her elbows. His gaze dropped and his breath caught. Lord, he was going to be late for work.

In the living room, his phone rang again. It was the tone he'd picked for Gabe.

"You going to get that?" she asked.

He gave her a slow shake of his head and returned her knowing smile.

"Good." She slipped on top of him, her breasts pressing to his bare chest. The heat of her touch made his entire body awaken.

Someone knocked on his front door. Clay's smile vanished as he sensed something was wrong. He took Izzie's shoulders and set her aside as he sat up.

"Stay here."

He slipped out of bed and into his jeans, then cast a look over his shoulder, surprised to see the worry in her face. She knelt on his bed, sheet clutched to her breasts and her other fist over her mouth. He was about to ask her what was wrong when the knock turned into a pounding.

"Clay?"

That was Gabe's voice.

"Open up."

He reached the door a moment later and pulled the door open to see Gabe wearing his uniform and a sour look.

"She here?" he asked, thumbing over his shoulder at Izzie's truck.

"Yeah."

"Get her."

Clay cocked his head. "Why?"

"I have to arrest her."

Chapter Seventeen

Rebranding. That was the charge against Izzie.

Clay stood aside as Gabe read Izzie her rights and then asked her if she had any questions. She was crying now and asked Clay to call her mother. Gabe put her in the back of his cruiser and closed the door. Clay grabbed his arm before his brother swung into the unit. Clay motioned with his head, and Gabe followed him a few feet from the vehicle.

"How did this happen?" asked Clay.

"Pizarro got a complaint of missing cattle. So he sent someone over to Izzie's place to do a count. There's a discrepancy in the number of the cattle she has and the number they released from quarantine."

"That doesn't make any sense. Who made the count?"

"Victor Bustros. Pizarro asked him to go over to Izzie's place."

Victor was the branding inspector for Black

He froze for only a moment before sweeping her up in his arms for a real kiss, the kind he'd been wanting to give her since the tenth grade.

Chapter Fifteen

Izzie's blood surged as Clay deepened the kiss. She pushed toward him and relished the hard pressure of his mouth on hers. His hand came up, gripping the back of her neck, and she let him take some of her weight. She lifted on her toes to get even closer, sliding her tongue against his. But he pulled away, setting her at arms' distance.

She was about to object, but then she heard the voices, other members of the community moving through the lot to their vehicles. How had she not even heard them? And why was it that he had?

Izzie had been completely lost in their kiss, and it irked her that Clay still had the wherewithal to notice what was going on around them. But she was grateful, too. She did not wish to be the subject of more gossip, mostly because the idea of facing something like what Clay had endured scared her to the core.

settled in against the cold stone and damp moss, she wondered if, like Geronimo, this would be her final stand. She understood now what it meant to fight against terrible odds for your family. Like those warriors of old, she fought because she was left with only two choices. Fight or die.

Izzie took the red bandanna from around her neck and folded it carefully. Then she tied it in the fashion of her people, like a male warrior would with a wide band tight across his forehead. She lifted her rifle and waited. From somewhere up-hill she heard a war whoop and knew Clay had engaged the enemy.

CLAY ALLOWED THEM to see him for just the briefest instant, not long enough, he hoped, to get a bead on him before he rushed away down the trail. He veered off before the first snare and was gratified to hear orders shouted in Spanish and then the heavy footfalls of pursuit. He watched as the first man caught his boot on the trip wire that sent the section of log he had suspended above them crashing down. It glanced off the first man's shoulder but struck the second of four squarely in the face. Clay winced at the crunch of wood splintering bone. The second man dropped to the trail. The third man fell to a knee and lifted his semiautomatic machine gun, scanning the area for a target and finding none. Clay had already dropped from view. He knew enough Spanish to understand that the downed man was alive and heard the order to leave him. Too bad. He had hoped they would order one of the three to carry him back to the SUV.

Clay waited until they had continued down the trail before retrieving the abandoned man, dragging him into the shrubs and tying him wrist to ankle in a series of knots Clay had learned from his brothers. He also knew from firsthand experience that the more the victim struggled, the tighter the knots became.

The men were moving cautiously now. So slowly that they might see the snare only a few feet before them. He had hidden the noose well, but the trip line had only some greenery disguising it. He knew that it would not fool any of his siblings, but the lead man, now inching carefully along, still placed his silver-tipped cowboy boot squarely in the noose, and a moment later he was rocketing into the air, his semiautomatic firing in a wild arc that sent his two remaining comrades diving for cover. One man landed close enough for Clay to disable him.

Clay did not like to cause pain, but all he needed to do was think of Izzie, just fifty yards down this very path, and it was easy to draw his knife and slice cleanly through the man's hamstring. The suspended man's howling was so loud, he wondered if the final man even heard Clay's victim's scream. Clay punched the blade of the knife into his other thigh and then relieved him of his guns. He left him howling and rolling from side to side under a bush beyond the edge of the trail.

The last remaining man was now trying to cut down his friend, which was a terrible idea. Likely the man would land on his head and break his neck. Clay sent the man running down the trail with a blast of gun fire. Less than a minute later he heard his screams and knew he had blundered into the spider web of monofilament and fishing hooks that Clay had rigged to come loose on contact.

He followed and reached the final man at the same time as Izzie. She trained her rifle on their foe as Clay ignored the hooks that tore the man's forehead, neck and body and quickly tied him.

By now the two men who had been left behind would be hearing the screams and cries of their comrades. They had no vehicle. These were not the men in charge. No, the leader was the coward who had abandoned his team at the first sign of trouble and run into the net. But still, Clay thought they would be coming. And he was out of traps.

IZZIE DID NOT want to leave Clay, but she thought his plan was a good one. With only two men left, it would be best if she could draw them from cover. Unlike Clay, she did not wish to bring them in alive. They were on her land. They were trying to kill her, and she was more than willing to protect her family and the man she loved.

An even match now, Clay said, with two of them and two cartel killers from Mexico. Two Apache versus two Comancheros. It was an old match, and each side had their share of victories and losses.

Clay wanted to get behind them. Izzie wanted to shoot them on open ground. But it was already too late for that, because when they retraced their path it was to discover that their attackers had already crossed the pasture and had reached cover. She saw their position, below them, hiding in the rocks. Clay had left two men disabled, howling in pain and shouting orders and threats at the remaining men. They were living decoys, but Clay needed time to get behind the approaching men. He took the semiautomatics. But he carried them across his back. What he carried in his hand was his knife and his rope. She had seen what he could do with that rope; she had watched him practicing his throw for hours. She had seen him ride at a full gallop, rope a calf, leap from his horse, flip the animal and rope its hind and forelegs all in less than five seconds.

But none of the calves he'd ever roped had carried guns.

One man was making his way between rocks. Clay told her to let them get closer, let them separate. Then keep them distracted and apart, so he could take them out. Had she given him enough time? They were only thirty feet below her now. One man moving and then the next. She needed to stop their advance. So she watched through her rifle scope as the first man made his next move, leaving the rocks for the more flimsy cover of a downed Ponderosa pine. Then she pulled the trigger, shooting high, and he predictably flattened to the ground. She sighted him, hoping for another shot. Her fury battled with her desire to follow Clay's orders. He wanted them alive.

The man stayed down for a long time. Then he shouted for his comrade and was answered by silence. He called again, a note of hysteria now entering his voice. But his partner did not reply. Izzie smiled. Clay had reached the other man.

The final man's voice was frantic now. He swore and called out in Spanish to the Virgin Mary. Izzie scowled.

"She won't help you," she called, and then closed one eye, watching for her chance. Behind him came the snap of a branch. Clay would never be so careless. The man lifted up and looked back, responding like a gopher to a whistle. Izzie pulled the trigger and heard the scream.

Then Clay leaped on the man. The man's gun flew into the air, and she saw Clay lace both hands together and bring them down hard. The woods went silent. Behind her came the cries of their leader, calling for his men, swearing vengeance and death as the hooks gaffed him like a trout. Beyond that came the sound of steady sobs. The one Clay had dispatched without killing him, she supposed. At the moment he did not seem grateful.

Clay stood and waved.

"All clear."

"Dead?" she asked.

"You got him in the shoulder. Good shot."

"I was aiming for his head." She scrambled down toward him.

"Oh," he said, regarding the man in question. "Bad shot."

She kept her rifle ready until she saw their attacker lying motionless, facedown, with his hands neatly secured behind his back. Blood welled through a hole in his jacket like a running stream.

Izzie let the rifle slip to her side as all the fight drained out of her. She began to shake and reached with her free arm. Clay pulled her close. Izzie let the sobs come.

"You're safe, Izzie. I've got you."

He had always gotten her, always been there.

"What if they send more?"

"With the FBI wise to the location of their cook site? With my brother patrolling this area?" He stroked his hand over her head. "With Tessay under arrest? No, Izzie. They won't be back."

Not here, anyway. But they would be back on the reservation. The protection of Indian land was just too tempting to the cartel, and the money was too enticing to some members of their tribe.

Izzie burrowed her face into the soft flannel of Clay's worn shirt and breathed in the warm reassurance of his scent. How had she ever made it so many years without him?

From somewhere below their line of sight came the sound of sirens. Clay's brother Gabe and likely his uncle, Agent Forrest, were on their way.

Clay set her back and took a long look at her, scrutinizing her face.

"You going to be all right?"

Her stomach dropped. Something about the way he said that made her think he was saying farewell. One look at his face and she knew the truth. What he was really asking was would she be all right without him?

"Yes," she whispered. "Or I will be."

He gave her a sad smile.

"Go on," she said, giving him permission to go.

Clay moved toward the open pasture. Waving

his arms toward the approaching police cruisers. She knew what he would do now that she was safe. He would leave her alone again, give her her privacy, let her keep her stellar reputation among the ranching community, because that was what she had always wanted. But she didn't want that now. Now she wanted Clay Cosen just as he was, because there wasn't a better man anywhere. The only trouble was, she didn't know if he wanted her.

Was it already too late? Had she hurt him too deeply and too often to ever make amends?

She watched Clay walk out to meet his brother and felt what Clay must have experienced when she walked away from him, a sense of hopeless loss. Izzie's breath shuddered as the tears came again.

Chapter Twenty-Three

Clay watched Gabe directing his men to wait and then ducked through the fencing. A moment later, he and their uncle came striding forward together in a perfect matched gait. They made an ominous sight, Gabe in his police uniform, gold tribal shield flashing in the sunlight, and Luke, dressed in a dark gray suit and tie that made him look every inch the G-man.

There was no easy way to tell his brother that he had fled the scene of a crime. Luckily, Gabe opened the conversation without waiting for him.

"She okay?"

Clay nodded.

"You okay?"

Another nod.

"I told you to stay put."

"Did you expect me to?"

Gabe's mouth quirked for just an instant as he struggled to keep hold of his stern expression.

"Did you pick up Tessay?" asked Clay.

"Not yet. Brought all the horses," he said, motioning toward the six cruisers that covered the 1,800 square miles of Apache reservation. He glanced back toward the woods, where Izzie emerged from the rocks leading her horses.

"I need you to call a vet. They shot Biscuit."

Gabe got on his radio. Then he rested a hand on his pistol as if it was the armrest of a familiar chair.

From the woods came howls of anger mingled with the high-pitched screams of pain. Luke and Gabe exchanged a look.

"Who's that?"

Clay went through it in sequence, the call from Rubin, finding his body. His conversation with Tribal Councilman Arnold Tessay and then coming to help Izzie face five cartel killers.

"How many dead?" asked Luke.

"None."

That made both men exchange a look. Gabe shook his head in clear disappointment, and his uncle cocked his head to stare at Clay.

"What?" asked Clay.

"You should shoot to kill," said Gabe, repeating what he knew from law enforcement. If you use your weapon, aim for mass.

Clay knew that philosophy. But he had a record. That made him see things differently.

"Very dangerous," said Luke.

"More witnesses for you," said Clay.

"Let's go mop up." Gabe lifted his radio. One of the cruisers headed up the mountain, to the improved road and the abandoned SUV.

Luke called his partner. She exited the car by the road, and Clay was struck with two things. She was small, and she was so blonde that her hair seemed to be a reflection of the sunlight.

"*That's* your partner?" asked Clay.

Luke glanced back. "Yeah. I know. But she's tougher than she looks."

"I sure hope so."

"Young. On her third assignment. Before that she was in US Army."

"Oh, boy," said Clay, knowing army and US Marines didn't always get along.

"It's okay. Let's go find some illegal aliens."

Clay walked them across the pasture where Izzie waited with Rocket and Biscuit, comforting the horses. Biscuit now stood with her front leg raised and her chest oozing blood.

After Clay had pointed out all the wriggling bodies of their attackers, Gabe took him into custody. Izzie left Biscuit the minute she saw Gabe put Clay in the back of his cruiser. It was the ride Clay had never wanted to take again, and this time Izzie was there to witness his humiliation. Somehow, despite all his efforts, he was in custody again. The look on Izzie's face made Clay feel sick. He read her expression as a kind of acceptance that he was what they all said, the black sheep, the black eye, the raw wound, the lost child or worse…just like his father.

Clay went through another round of questioning at the station. Gabe told him all the men he'd captured would live and that Luke and his partner, Agent Walker, had taken custody of them. He also told him that Clyne had called a special meeting of the tribal council and that Tessay had been suspended pending investigation. It seemed that Arnold's prediction was wrong. The federal and local law did not take his word at face value and were investigating Rubin's death with Tessay as the prime suspect.

Clyne appeared after the meeting at police headquarters with an attorney for Clay, whom Gabe said he didn't need. It was a rare instance when his two older brothers disagreed. Clyne won the argument, as usual, and Clay's new attorney began the process of securing Clay's release on bail, which Clyne generously posted.

Clay was released to Clyne's custody, and he picked up his personal items at the main desk to discover Izzie had called twice. He didn't call back. He was too tired and his heart was too sore to hear her goodbye.

He had a late meal with Clyne and his grandmother; Gabe and Luke were too busy to make an appearance. He'd never gotten a chance to move his things here, so he returned to his place, and it was not until he hit the shower that the exhaustion really took hold. He barely got dried off before he stretched out on the couch and was out as if someone hit him on the head.

On Sunday morning, he woke to the far off buzzing of the alarm in his old bedroom because he had forgotten to turn it off. He groaned and buried his face under the sofa pillow until he recalled that Izzie regularly attended church. That got him up and moving. He threw his packed possessions into his truck. It was discouraging that everything but his saddle fit in only two large duffels and a single box. He made it to his grandmother's in time to join her and his brothers for services. But he was disappointed to find Izzie was not in attendance. Her brothers and mother were there, and her mother seemed to spend the entire service staring at Clay in stony silence and then formally thanked him for saving her daughter's life. It was the most awkward moment of his life, followed by the next as Clay accepted the offered kiss on the cheek and then excused himself, leaving his grandmother and Izzie's mother deep in conversation.

On Monday, Clay was back at work and was surprised when his boss told Clay that he was proud of him. On Tuesday, Gabe arrested Boone

Pizarro. According to Donner, the shamed councillor implicated Pizarro while looking for a plea deal. Pizarro was accused both of rebranding Izzie's cattle and ordering Victor Bustros to check Izzie's cattle's brands. No charges were made against Bustros yet.

Wednesday morning Clay's new attorney stopped by his work to tell him the forensics came back on Rubin's murder. Clay's prints were all over the murder weapon, which was bad, of course. But a partial print of Arnold Tessay's was found on one of the empty bullet casings at the scene. It was enough to hold Tessay, who had secured a defense attorney, a "damned good one" who had already requested a bail hearing.

Clay wondered if Tessay would get it because he'd heard his uncle Luke predict Tessay was a flight risk and, if allowed bail, might flee, but perhaps that was because Luke was hoping he would run. Leaving the reservation meant Tessay would lose his protected status. Clay knew that Luke and his partner were building a federal case against him, which he would present for the tribal council's approval and, if successful, press the district attorney to accept the case.

Clyne showed up on Wednesday evening to take him to the closed session of tribal council and told him that their youngest brother, Kino, and his new wife, Lea, were due home tomorrow.

"Ready?" asked Clyne.

"Yeah." They climbed into his older brother's SUV, but Clyne didn't start up the vehicle.

Clay lifted his brows in an unspoken question.

Clyne drummed his fingers on the wheel. "She's speaking to the tribal council tonight, same as you."

He didn't need to ask who *she* was. Izzie. He'd see her. It would be hard, as hard as every chance meeting he had suffered through since his return from the detention center in Colorado.

But when he entered the council chambers, it was worse than he imagined. He saw her. No, he *felt* her. Just being in the same room caused a physical pain in his chest. He rubbed his knuckles over his sternum, but it only got worse.

Izzie stood when he entered and walked down the center aisle to meet him. His shoulders went tight as if every muscle there had suddenly seized up. He clenched his jaw, and sweat rose on his brow.

Before him most of the tribal council were already seated. The council members, minus Arnold Tessay, sat on one side of the table. Their chairman, Ralph Siqueria, had returned from DC and presided over the closed session with only invited speakers. Gabe, Luke, his blonde partner and Izzie all sat on the opposite side of the table but pivoted as Clyne and Clay entered.

Izzie waited as Clay approached. He didn't know what kept him moving.

"Hello, Clay," she said.

He nodded, hoping to move past her to his seat, but she blocked his path.

Clay glanced to the witnesses and grimaced. They all sat motionless as if afraid to miss a moment of this personal drama.

"You've been avoiding me," said Izzie.

"That's so."

"Why?"

"Izzie, let's just get through this?"

She shook her head. "Not until I tell you something."

He gazed down at her soft brown eyes, taking in the image of her pointed chin and the angle of her brow and her smooth skin and, well, everything that made her so beautiful. In that moment he had time to consider all the mistakes that kept him from being what she needed. Clyne took his seat across from Gabe. Clay looked at his older brothers. Their presence seemed to mock him. Neither of his brothers had let their mother's tragic death or their father's train wreck of a life derail theirs.

"Are you listening to me?" she asked.

Had she been speaking? His face went hot. He wished she would not do this now, so publicly. But perhaps she wanted all to know she was grateful and their business was finished. He could bear it. Couldn't he?

"Clay, I said that I made mistakes. That I let my obligations and the opinions of others keep me from doing what *I* wanted. But I won't let that happen anymore. It is *my* life and *my* decision what man I choose to share it with."

Clay wrinkled his brow in confusion. This was not the speech he had expected to hear.

"I don't understand."

"When I was young, I listened to my mother. I pretended to avoid you, but I went out with Martin just to be near you. When he died, I didn't grieve for him. I grieved for you and for us, and that shames me. Then when you came back, I was so certain that I had to fulfill my promise to my father and to keep the herd for my brothers before I even considered a family of my own."

Clay's heart was beating so fast that his ribs ached.

"I understand, Mizz Nosie."

Izzie stamped her foot. "Don't you dare call me that. Not after the night we spent together."

His gaze snapped to hers. Behind him, he heard the intake of breath from someone on the council. Was that Clyne, shocked at Izzie's admission?

Why would she tell them all? She had always guarded her reputation. An Apache woman's virtue was important. Her honor like a living thing, to be nurtured…but she had told them all—publicly.

He scrutinized her face, but she had adopted the blank expression of a woman who did not wish to reveal her emotions. He felt the first stirring of hope. She had stood here before her tribal leadership and told them, every one of them, what they had done.

She must have lost her mind. He tried to control the damage.

"It was the fear, the need, that's all."

"No." She grabbed the front of his shirt, bunching it in her fists, and gave him a little shake. But she didn't need to, because she had his full attention. "It was not the fear or the need. I am not ashamed of you. I am ashamed of myself. I am proud of you. You are brave, honest, smart. You put the needs of everyone first. You helped Kino down on the border, and you are giving up your place so he can make a home there with his wife. You helped Gabe and your uncle solve this case. And you kept me alive."

His breathing was so fast that he was dizzy with it. He had to widen his stance just to regain his equilibrium.

"Bella?"

"I love you, Clay Cosen. I have loved you since I was a little girl, and I will love you all my life."

He looked at her, trying to understand what was happening, afraid to believe his ears. She nodded, confirming what she had said.

"I love you," she whispered.

She said that here, aloud before the entire tribal council. Clay's jaw dropped as he looked from one smiling face to the next.

She loved him.

"Clay, can you ever forgive me?"

The buzzing in his ears silenced all sound. He could not hear the men and women behind him at the council table, because his senses were too full of Isabella Nosie.

And possibilities.

"Is it true?" he asked.

"I love you so much."

He turned to his brothers, his voice hushed with astonishment. Clyne was wiping at his eyes, and Gabe had puffed up like a Tom turkey.

"She loves me," he said to them.

Clyne called for a recess.

Several of the council members glanced at Clay and Izzie as they rose and made their way out of the chamber.

IZZIE STARED AT Clay, but he just stood there with a stunned look on his face. She had bared her soul to him, and he was silent as the room in which they stood.

Was this how he had felt after the shame of his arrest, standing in the judicial chamber? What if he didn't love her? What if she had waited too long? What if he could not forget, could not forgive?

Her cheeks burned with shame. Why should he forgive her? She had done nothing to earn his love.

"You said that in front of everybody. The entire council."

"I know. I'm sorry. I just—just…" She was a fool. "I wanted everyone to know." She dropped her gaze. "I didn't mean to embarrass you."

She stared up at him, willing her lower lip to cease its trembling. He remained silent, and she could not read his thoughts. All she knew was that she was too late.

It was hard to speak now. The pain lodged in her throat like a wedge, choking her. There was no saving face, no way to keep her pride. She had taken the risk and lost.

"I'd understand if you can't forgive me. I was so caught up in what my father wanted and what my mother wanted that I lost sight of us."

She sank into the closest seat, set up for the public meetings. Clay dropped to a knee before her.

He took her hand and gave a little squeeze. "Izzie, look at me."

She did.

"There is nothing to forgive. You took care of your family. And I repaid my debt for the mistake."

"But you didn't make a mistake."

"I trusted Martin. I knew him well enough to know he wanted that two hundred dollars. I even knew him well enough to recognize the lengths he'd go in order to get it. That alone was worth eighteen months in detention. As for us, well, most folks can't look past a single mistake. But you did."

"Oh, Clay."

"And I love you for that. I love you, Isabella. I've loved you since I was ten years old. And I want you to be my wife."

"Your wife?" Now she was the one staring in shock.

He smiled and brought the back of her hand to his mouth brushing his lips against sensitive skin.

"Would you like time to think about it?" he asked.

She shook her head. "No. I've had too much time to think. Too much time away from you."

"So…?" His mouth quirked.

She threw herself into his arms, nodding her head against the warm strength of his neck and shoulder.

"Yes, Clay. I will be your wife."

Chapter Twenty-Four

The following Sunday afternoon preparations were well underway for the barbecue lunch following church to welcome home the newlyweds. When his grandmother had mentioned her plans for the gathering to Clay, he had immediately asked if he could invite Izzie.

"She's your girl, isn't she?" Glendora had replied and then insisted that he invite Isabella's entire family.

His girl. He liked the sound of that.

Because of Gabe's investigation and Clyne's political responsibilities, this was the first time the brothers had all been together since Kino's wedding.

Clay joined his older brothers at the fire pit in the backyard. They had the smoker going, coals ready. The ribs, rubbed with a mix of seasoning, waited in the cooler.

Their uncle was, unfortunately, unable to attend. Gabe said they had leads to follow, thanks to the suspects they had in custody. Of course, the men were not talking, but Luke knew which cartel they belonged with. The FBI was anxious to cut this supply line while the trail was hot.

Gabe said they had some new leads to follow because both Tessay and Pizarro were now anxious to cooperate to avoid federal prosecution.

All three brothers turned at the sound of tires crunching in the gravel drive beside the house. There was Kino's truck pulling to a stop. Glendora hurried out of the house and rushed past them, hugging Lea, who looked rosy-cheeked and happier than Clay had ever seen her. After Glendora had hugged Kino, she captured his bride and left her youngest grandson to his brothers. The men hugged and slapped each other on the back.

"Any more news?" asked Gabe, ever the investigator. He was referring to the hunt for their missing sister.

"Yes, actually. Grandma is going to flip. You know I spoke to Jovanna's case manager."

Clay didn't know. Somehow he'd missed that piece of news in all the excitement of the past two weeks.

"Well, after the foster home closed, she handled Jovanna's placement in a temporary foster home and then her permanent adoption." Kino turned to Clyne. "I did what you said. I hired an attorney up there, and he has filed papers to get the adoption unsealed. He says that's the first step, and then we can seek to have the adoption overturned." Kino drew out three business cards from his front pocket. "Here is his name."

Gabe accepted a card and passed the other cards to Clay and Clyne.

"He said there will be a hearing. One of us should go."

"I'll go," said Clay. They all looked at him. Clyne and Gabe had been up there already, and Gabe was in the middle of investigating the biggest case of his career. Clyne had council business, including electing a new member to replace the vacancy left by Tessay's resignation. Kino had spent much of his honeymoon tracking Jovanna through the foster-care system. It was Clay's turn to help find their baby sister.

The brothers turned to Clyne, who nodded his approval.

"How long will it take to get her back?" asked Gabe.

"I don't know," said Kino.

"Better be before this July. Grandma has her dress half done. She's beading the yoke every day."

"And she's already spoken to the shaman," added Clyne.

"We're going to need another cow," said Clay.

"Who will be her sponsor?" asked Clyne. It

was a position of honor, but one only an Apache woman and member of Jovanna's tribe could fill. It was customary for this to be a close friend of the family. This woman would act as both teacher and guide. The brothers looked blankly at each other for a moment.

"We have to find her first," reminded Clay.

"We'll get it done somehow," said Clyne. "Grandma's not the only one who wants her back. We all do. She's our sister, and she belongs here with her people."

"One more thing," said Kino. "The case manager slipped up. She said that Jovanna's parents weren't Indian."

"What!" roared Clyne.

"They're white?" asked Gabe.

"I don't know. Maybe. Not Indian, that's all he said."

"What does that mean?" asked Gabe.

"It means they're not Indian," said Clyne. "We have to get her home. Now!"

Clay had seen that look before. Clyne would not rest until he retrieved Jovanna.

Their eldest brother was a staunch advocate for Indian children being raised in their communities. Especially since so many Indian children had been removed from their families and lost to their culture.

"We need a court order," reminded Gabe.

Kino placed a hand on Clay's shoulder. "I heard you and Izzie are back together."

"Yeah." Clay grinned. He was so happy. The only dark spot in his world right now was his baby sister's absence.

"About time. You going to marry her?" asked Kino.

His brother was always blunt, and only he could get away with it.

Clyne and Gabe exchanged a glance. They always seemed to know what the other was thinking.

Clay shrugged. "I already asked her."

"And," said Gabe.

"She said yes."

Kino gave a whoop of excitement. The brothers clapped Clay on the back.

"Have you got a ring?" asked Clyne, ever the practical one.

"Not yet."

"I have Mom's," said Clyne.

The brothers went silent as Clyne opened his shirt, revealing the traditional medicine bundle carried by warriors of old. Inside were items of power, and the contents of each man's bundle was private. They had each made such a packet as part of their education in the tribe. Both Clyne and Gabe wore theirs about their necks. Gabe now pressed a hand over his, making Clay curious as to what the leather pouch contained. Meanwhile, Clyne drew his over his head and opened it. A moment later he held their mother's diamond solitaire ring between his thumb and forefinger.

Clay felt the lump in his throat. His brother had carried this next to his heart for all these years. The ring his father had given his mother with his promise. A promise he did not keep. Clay knew that he would not ask Izzie to wear that ring.

"That should go to *your* wife," said Clay.

Gabe nodded his agreement.

"I don't think I will marry. There is no one." He shrugged.

"That's because you want to marry the next Miss Apache Nation," said Gabe, but his kidding tone gained only a scowl from Clyne.

"How are we going to survive as a people, if we don't marry other Indians? We've got a culture to preserve and a responsibility."

It was another thing Clyne felt very strongly about, the survival of the Apache people.

"Then you better get married and have lots of Apache kids," said Kino.

Clyne made a noncommittal sound and tucked the ring back into his pouch.

Gabe clapped a hand on Clay's shoulder. "Does Grandmother know yet?"

"We told her."

"What kind of wedding?" asked Gabe.

"Small, soon."

"And you'll return to work with Donner?" asked Clyne.

"Not sure. Izzie will need help with her cattle for a while. Until the boys are old enough to handle them."

"Will you live there?"

Clay shook his head. "We want our own place."

"There is a position open on the tribal council," said Clyne.

Clay turned to Gabe to see his response, and then he realized Clyne was speaking to him. Clay laughed, thinking they were teasing him. Neither of his older brothers smiled.

"Me?" he said, pressing a finger into his chest. "They don't want me."

"Actually several of the council have approached me and asked me to speak to you about this. People of the tribe are all talking about you and your courage. Your heroism has gotten you noticed."

Clay blinked in astonishment. "Me," he said with wonder. He realized that he had lost many things the day of the robbery—his pride, his friends—but never his integrity and never his family. Izzie had believed in him, though he didn't know it at the time. Now others did, as well. Most importantly he believed in himself.

He grinned. "Let me talk it over with Izzie."

The brothers laughed and slapped him on the back.

"I want to hear all about what happened," said Kino. "Everything! I already heard Gabe's version, but he makes everything sound like a police report."

"I gave you the facts," said Gabe.

Izzie pulled into the drive with her mother. A moment later her two brothers spilled out of the backseat. They seemed to grow by the minute.

"Later," said Clay, and went to meet them.

He approached with his hands in his pockets, not sure how to greet her. He wanted to sweep her up in his arms for a kiss, but with Carol and her brothers here, he was uncertain.

Izzie came bounding forward, keys jangling in her hand as she leaped into his arms and kissed him on the mouth in front of his brothers, her brothers and her mother. Clay froze for just a moment, and then he did what he had dreamed of doing all day. He kissed her back, hard and possessive. Her mouth was soft and yielding and full of promises he intended to see she kept.

Someone cleared his throat. Clay stepped back, and Izzie moved away, grinning up at him with such pride and love it made his chest swell. His brothers stood behind him, as they always had. Her brothers stood behind her.

Glendora moved between the two groups and took Izzie in her arms for an enveloping hug.

"It is so good to have you back at my table, Isabella." Then Glendora turned to Izzie's mother, relieving her of the large casserole she gripped. Glendora passed the glass container to Clay and then looped her arm with Izzie's mom, steering her toward the house as if the gathering was completely natural. Clay and Izzie shared a smile.

His brothers parted to let the two older women pass.

"I hear that my grandson has asked for your daughter's hand."

"He asked me for her hand," said Carol, which was true. Somehow he and Carol Nosie had both survived that awkward conversation and he had gained her mother's guarded consent.

Clay could not hear some of the reply, but then his grandmother's words were clear.

"Too long coming, I say."

"A good match," said Carol.

Clay felt he could breathe again, and Izzie beamed up at him.

"I told you," she whispered.

Clay wrapped an arm around Izzie. It was the gift he had most wanted, her mother's approval. The men headed for the fire pit to put the ribs on the coals. Izzie's brothers hesitated between Izzie and the men.

Clay motioned the two after his brothers. "Go on."

The two bounded off like deer joining the herd.

Izzie squeezed his hand. "Did you tell your brothers?"

"Yes."

"And?" she asked.

"They're happy. Said it was about time."

She laughed. "And they're right about that."

"Izzie? I have something to ask you."

She turned, her dark brows lifted in the middle like the wings of a perching bird. "Yes."

"Clyne says, that is, he's been asked by the council if I would be interested in seeking a place on the tribal council."

"Tessay's place?" she asked.

"You don't sound surprised," he said.

"Surprised? That they would pick a hero? A man of great integrity? Clay, you deserve this. Don't you know that?"

"I'm beginning to. What do you think?"

"It will be hard work, but I don't know anyone who could represent our tribe better than you."

He warmed under the glow of her faith in him.

"You approve?" he asked.

"Yes, and I am so proud of you."

He kissed her again, there on the land that had

belonged to their people for longer than memory. Here in the shadow of the sacred Black Mountains where they would make a home and build a life—together.

* * * * *

LARGER-PRINT BOOKS!

HARLEQUIN

Presents®

GET 2 FREE LARGER-PRINT NOVELS PLUS 2 FREE GIFTS!

YES! Please send me 2 FREE LARGER-PRINT Harlequin Presents® novels and my 2 FREE gifts (gifts are worth about $10). After receiving them, if I don't wish to receive any more books, I can return the shipping statement marked "cancel." If I don't cancel, I will receive 6 brand-new novels every month and be billed just $5.30 per book in the U.S. or $5.74 per book in Canada. That's a saving of at least 12% off the cover price! It's quite a bargain! Shipping and handling is just 50¢ per book in the U.S. and 75¢ per book in Canada.* I understand that accepting the 2 free books and gifts places me under no obligation to buy anything. I can always return a shipment and cancel at any time. Even if I never buy another book, the two free books and gifts are mine to keep forever.

176/376 HDN GHVY

Name	(PLEASE PRINT)	
Address		Apt. #
City	State/Prov.	Zip/Postal Code

Signature (if under 18, a parent or guardian must sign)

Mail to the **Reader Service:**
IN U.S.A.: P.O. Box 1867, Buffalo, NY 14240-1867
IN CANADA: P.O. Box 609, Fort Erie, Ontario L2A 5X3

Are you a subscriber to Harlequin Presents® books and want to receive the larger-print edition?
Call 1-800-873-8635 today or visit us at www.ReaderService.com.

* Terms and prices subject to change without notice. Prices do not include applicable taxes. Sales tax applicable in N.Y. Canadian residents will be charged applicable taxes. Offer not valid in Quebec. This offer is limited to one order per household. Not valid for current subscribers to Harlequin Presents Larger-Print books. All orders subject to credit approval. Credit or debit balances in a customer's account(s) may be offset by any other outstanding balance owed by or to the customer. Please allow 4 to 6 weeks for delivery. Offer available while quantities last.

Your Privacy—The Reader Service is committed to protecting your privacy. Our Privacy Policy is available online at www.ReaderService.com or upon request from the Reader Service.

We make a portion of our mailing list available to reputable third parties that offer products we believe may interest you. If you prefer that we not exchange your name with third parties, or if you wish to clarify or modify your communication preferences, please visit us at www.ReaderService.com/consumerschoice or write to us at Reader Service Preference Service, P.O. Box 9062, Buffalo, NY 14240-9062. Include your complete name and address.

HPLP15

LARGER-PRINT BOOKS!

GET 2 FREE LARGER-PRINT NOVELS PLUS
2 FREE GIFTS!

❧ HARLEQUIN®

Romance

From the Heart, For the Heart

HRLP15

LARGER-PRINT BOOKS!
GET 2 FREE LARGER-PRINT NOVELS PLUS
2 FREE GIFTS!

HARLEQUIN®

super romance®

More Story...More Romance

HSRLP15

YES! Please send me **The Montana Mavericks Collection** in Larger Print.

This collection begins with 3 FREE books and 2 FREE gifts (gifts valued at approx. $20.00 retail) in the first shipment, along with the other first 4 books from the collection! If I do not cancel, I will receive 8 monthly shipments until I have the entire 51-book Montana Mavericks collection. I will receive 2 or 3 FREE books in each shipment and I will pay just $4.99 US/ $5.89 CDN for each of the other four books in each shipment, plus $2.99 for shipping and handling per shipment.*If I decide to keep the entire collection, I'll have paid for only 32 books, because 19 books are FREE! I understand that accepting the 3 free books and gifts places me under no obligation to buy anything. I can always return a shipment and cancel at any time. My free books and gifts are mine to keep no matter what I decide.

263 HCN 2404   463 HCN 2404

Name	(PLEASE PRINT)	
Address		Apt. #
City	State/Prov.	Zip/Postal Code

Signature (if under 18, a parent or guardian must sign)

Mail to the **Reader Service:**
IN U.S.A.: P.O. Box 1867, Buffalo, NY 14240-1867
IN CANADA: P.O. Box 609, Fort Erie, Ontario L2A 5X3